The *Uneasy* Series

Volume I

BLOOD AND BONE

A Smattering of Unease

Shannon Rae Noble

The *Uneasy* Series Volume I
Blood and Bone:
A Smattering of Unease

Published by Crow 99 Books

Cover image by Shannon Rae Noble
Cover design by Bells Design
Contributing editors Brett Bottoff & Chirico Designs
Logo by Chirico Designs

ISBN 978-0-692-70663-3

Critique provided by Lansing Writers Group
Beta readers: Chris Furst & James Derry

For Nik and Dawn, because they believe in me.

CONTENTS

BLOOD AND BONE

Dusk had fallen. Clouds and the overhead foliage hid the rising moon and the stars that would just be appearing in the night sky.

Glory moved along the South Path of the Cross between the thick trees, her cloak secured close around her. In her left hand she carried the basket; in her right, she held a torch high to light the path in front of her.

She had great respect for the Wandering Wood. It was legendary for the creatures that inhabited it, together with its habit of "wandering" to different locations across the countryside; not to mention the many disappearances of travelers who were believed to have stepped off the Paths. Glory always stayed on the Paths and had never gotten lost.

When she reached the Cross at the heart of Wandering Wood, Glory stopped beside a nearby tree. She extinguished the torch and dug its handle into the rocky soil until the torch stood upright within easy reach. She set the basket on the ground, keeping it hidden behind the bottom folds of her black cloak. She pulled the hood forward to shadow her face. Then she stepped back and melted into a wide dip in the tree, becoming all but invisible. Here, she could watch the Cross without being noticed.

A crisp autumn breeze rustled through the Wood, and the few leaves still left on the trees whispered to one another in papery voices. The sound of snapping branches echoed now and again as animals both large and small moved through the darkness.

When the occasional small animal came to sniff curiously at Glory's feet, she hissed or kicked at it to send it running off through the trees. Otherwise she stood, waiting patiently.

From the North Path of the Cross came the sound of someone's approach. Hoof beats and the creak of an old wooden wagon. She sniffed the air. The scent was similar to her grandmother's musty smell, but Glory knew that it wasn't her.

She stayed still and silent within the gentle curve of the tree. She knew these people, but was loathe to speak with them.

The horses and wagon stopped at the Cross.

"Well met, young Glory!" called a voice as creaky as the wagon. "Why don't you come out and greet your Granny's oldest and best friends?"

Sighing, Glory took one step forward. Before setting out this evening, she had ingested a foul tasting herb concoction that was supposed to disguise the smell of her warm blood – but there was no remedy in the world that she could use to disguise her scent from one of her own.

"Good evening, Ladies," she said to Suluya and Loriana, the two white-haired crones who sat, side by side, on the bench seat.

"Are you on about Louisa's business tonight, then?" Suluya asked.

"You know that I am," Glory responded.

"Good girl. You do know that she needs you more than ever, now."

"Yes, ma'am."

"We wish you many blessings and courage to achieve the task at hand. But we must move along," said Loriana.

"I understand. Thank you, and blessings upon you, as well."

The horses resumed their steady pace and the wagon bearing the crones disappeared down the South Path of the Cross.

Glory sank back into the shadows of her tree.

As time passed, she watched travelers move through the Wood. The few humans she saw walked or rode past quickly, staying to their Path of the Cross. Those creatures native to the Wood didn't care about the Paths of the Cross and moved about as they pleased. Glory stayed in her spot, unnoticed, and let them go about their business.

She experienced a few anxious moments when a sickly-looking vampire type passed within a few feet of her hiding place. She had no wish to face the thing, and held her breath as it came within arm's reach. The herb concoction she had swallowed before setting out must be working, because the vampire floated on, unblinking.

Eventually, a rank, unclean smell drifted to her along the North Path of the Cross. She listened and sniffed, inhaling deeply. A horse. Carrying a man. Soon after, she heard the horse's hoof beats.

The man stopped his horse when they reached the Cross. He dismounted and led the horse directly to Glory.

"Good evening," he said.

You must be joking, Glory thought. *How did he detect me? Even the vampire didn't notice me.* She just looked at him. Her nostrils flared with the unpleasant odor that floated off of him in waves.

The man scratched his cheek, looked around, and tried again. "May I ask how a young woman such as yourself comes to be standing at the heart of Wandering Wood so late at night?"

"You may, though it's none of your business. I walked here," she snapped. She couldn't afford the niceties of courtesy. She needed to get rid of him, or her mission would be lost.

The man tipped his head back and laughed, white teeth flashing in the darkness. "Wandering Wood at such a dangerous hour is no place for a young lady. Please let me escort you out."

If she hadn't been on such an urgent and long-planned mission, and had the man's body been more recently bathed, Glory might have considered it. Her vision had grown accustomed to the darkness, and from what she could discern, he was well-built, and though his face was deeply lined and rough with stubble, he was pleasant enough to look at. But he had an ordinary heart. The creature she lay in wait for had an extraordinary heart.

"I am over the age to which curfew applies. I thank you for your offer, but I am waiting for another," she told him.

His face fell with disappointment. Glory paid it no mind. She was sure he would find another woman at the nearest tavern as soon as he exited the Wood.

His horse whickered and stamped nervously. The man looked into the surrounding trees and said, "Would you mind then, if I waited here a while with you? I would rather see you safe than just leave you here, knowing what walks Wandering Wood."

Irritation gnawed at Glory's nerves. She wished he would just stop talking. His repetition of the words "Wandering Wood" was insufferable, and his smell was starting to nauseate her.

"Are you, perhaps, a bard?" She asked him. "Where is your harp? Or do you travel with a lute?"

He just laughed again. Glory rolled her eyes in annoyance when he tethered his horse to a low tree branch.

A sudden sharp gust of wind caught Glory's cloak and blew it aside, exposing the basket at her feet. She quickly drew the cloak about her again.

The man raised his eyebrows. "So are you the young lady much talked of throughout the countryside? The girl who travels through the Wood with a basket of goodies for her sick grandmother?"

"You must have me confused with my cousin. She is known by the red cloak she wears. As you can see, mine is not red. It's black."

"Mmmm." He scrutinized her. "But it isn't every girl who carries a basket through the woods."

"I'm sure Miss Red isn't the only girl that's ever had a picnic in the woods! And the goodies I carry in my basket are *not* baked." Glory's thin patience had worn through. "Who *are* you, anyway? Don't you have somewhere to be?"

"Oh, I apologize for failing to introduce myself. My name is Gabriel Asphodel." He doffed his cap and bowed low. A wave of sickly body odor wafted with his movement. "You may call me Gabe. I am just passing through, in no real hurry to be anywhere, and I thought you might be glad of companionship." He reached out to put a hand on her arm.

The clouds above the wood suddenly parted, and the full moon's light shone down and lit the Cross. A long howl sounded through the Wood.

Glory's body tensed, filling with a sense of urgency. She could feel that her moment was swiftly drawing nigh. She needed to get rid of Gabe Asphodel.

"Surely you don't mind my . . . offer . . . o-of c-c-c-ompanion . . . ship . . ." His speech had become slurred, spoken between gritted teeth, and his breath was labored.

Glory pulled away from him. "Are you okay?"

"I . . . I . . . AAUUUGHHHH!" He raised both hands to his head. His horse whinnied and reared, pulling at the branch to which it was tethered.

"What's wrong? What's happening?"

Gabe Asphodel let out an agonized scream, and Glory watched as his fingers stretched, the nails growing into long, curved claws. His facial features melted, his nose elongated, and his ears grew into points. His arms and legs burst with huge muscles as his clothing ripped apart to accommodate the new growth.

He screamed again, and the scream grew into a long howl. His horse shrieked and reared again, snapping the branch it was tied to. The animal bolted, dragging the branch behind it.

Glory stood there for a second, then reached quickly for her basket. *This is it! Gabe Asphodel is the creature!*

She yanked a huge silver chain, collar, and muzzle out of the basket as Gabe fell to the ground and writhed. If she didn't do the deed now, during the throes of his transformation, he would kill her.

She dropped to her knees beside him, snapped the collar around his neck, and fought to slip the muzzle over his jaw, trying to avoid his sharp teeth as his head whipped back and forth. She tightened it as well as she could, pulling the silver strap around the back of his head. A sharp pain shot through her back as she struggled to roll his heavy body. Sweat broke across her brow as she managed to work the chain all the way around his torso, bracing her foot against his side so that she could pull it tight, ducking below his flailing arms.

The knuckles of one of his hands hit her in the ear. She gasped, stunned with the sudden pain and ringing in her ear.

She pushed through it and kept working. The silver was finally taking effect, diminishing the beast's strength. Tying his legs was an easier task.

Glory fell back, breathing heavily, her body bathed in sweat beneath her leather armor and heavy cloak. The creature looked at Glory with baleful yellow eyes, snarling against the muzzle, saliva dripping from its long fangs.

A shudder skittered down her back. She reached into the picnic basket and retrieved a long silver knife. She pulled it from its sheath, and the beast began to struggle against its chains. Glory heard the links creak, then *snap!* as the first one gave. Silver's magical properties were was much stronger against the beast than anything else.

Unfortunately, silver was short work against pure brute strength.

She had only a few short seconds to finish the job before both the chains and the muzzle broke into pieces.

She kissed the blade, and a blue glow rose from the silver. She knelt down and plunged it deep into the center of the monster's chest. The breast bone offered no more resistance than would a clot of butter. She cut a wide circle, while at the same time, her body trembling with effort, she tried to use her slight weight to hold down the beast's bucking body. She gagged at the foul smell. She worked on grimly. She didn't have time to vomit.

SNAP! SNAP! SNAP! SNAPSNAPSNAP! Silver links burst apart beneath her. Though the knife cut easily through the rib bones, the beast's struggles kept dislodging the knife from the cut. The thing's hot, rancid breath blew into her face, making her eyes water. She could see the lethal fangs from the corner of one eye. The damaged muzzle hung from its jaw.

She shoved the knife deep and pushed down on the handle, leveraging the blade upward, lifting out the roughly round piece of flesh and bone she had cut. She tossed the blade aside and plunged her hand into the cavity. With all her strength, she twisted and wrenched the heart from its thick, sinewy resting place. As it came free, the creature lunged and Glory fell backward, the hot, slimy muscle still beating in her hand.

The monster's long snout and fangs hovered over Glory's face, and her own heart nearly stopped in fear. The bright yellow eyes stared into her own. A long rope of sticky saliva dripped onto her cheek, where it stung and burned into her skin. She turned her head in disgust, and the beast's eyes glazed over. Its body landed heavily upon her chest, knocking the wind out of her.

Glory lay there, paralyzed in terror, not realizing for a moment that the beast was dead. When it remained unmoving, she stayed, sweating and panting, trying to calm the pounding in her chest.

After a few moments, she struggled to push the beast's body off her and wriggled herself from beneath its weight. Finally free, she sat up, wiped the string of the beast's saliva from her cheek, and clambered to her feet. Her legs felt like rubber, and she swayed drunkenly, waiting for the dizziness to recede.

She looked at the bloody naked human body lying on the ground before her. It was a shame. He hadn't been half-bad looking. And it turned out that Gabe Asphodel *did* have the extraordinary heart that would fulfill her needs. She squatted and pushed the man's body off the path and into the underbrush. The denizens of the Wood would take care of it.

She glanced around her furtively. There were no creatures nearby that had witnessed the killing, nor humans on any of the Paths of the Cross.

She lit her torch, then reached into her basket. She pulled out her extra cloak and removed the false bottom from the basket. She buried the now-stilled heart in the pile of melting slivered ice, then replaced the false bottom.

Her hands, her cloak, and no doubt her face, were covered in gore. She peeled off her cloak and dumped water from the skin attached to her belt onto a clean corner of the fabric. She scrubbed at her face, hands, and leather armor as best she could by the waning light of her torch. She found her knife where she had tossed it on the ground and sheathed it after she wiped it clean. She balled up the dirty cloak and put it in the basket. She would burn it later.

She gathered up what she could of the chain, collar, and muzzle, dropping the pieces into the basket. She covered herself with her spare cloak, pulling the red hood up over her blonde curls, where it fell forward and obscured her face.

She picked up the basket and moved quickly down the South Path of the Cross. The whole incident had taken less than ten minutes. It wasn't yet midnight.

Wouldn't Grandmother Louisa be pleased! And Suluya . . . and Loriana. Tomorrow evening they would dine on the heart of a lycanthrope. Grandmother Louisa's health would be restored, and she and her old crone friends would gain their youth back.

And Glory would retain her own youth - forever.

SIREN SCREAM

Troy cut the motor and steered *Harmony* carefully into the boathouse beside *Melody*. Thanks to a good morning's catch, he would be dining on fresh swordfish and prawns this evening.

Independent island living had made him a skilled fisherman.

He hefted the ice-filled chests, one at a time, onto the boards. He lowered his "walk" from the edge of the boat to the boards and guided his chair across. He secured the boat, but not too tightly. He gave both of his boats a once-over, making sure he had done all he could to prevent damage from the storm that the weather reports promised was blowing toward the island. He pulled the ocean-facing doors closed and dropped the latch.

He loaded the chests into the back compartment of his buggy and left the chair open inside the secured boathouse. He powered the buggy up the boardwalk across the beach to his house.

Once inside, he refrigerated his catch. He had already cleaned and cut steaks from the swordfish on the boat, dumping the remnants back into the ocean.

The morning's activity had whetted Troy's appetite. He prepared his breakfast and took it out to the deck.

He scanned the horizon with his binoculars. All was clear as far as he could see. There was just a hint of haze where the blue sky met the deeper blue of the ocean, many miles off in the distance. No sign yet of the approaching tropical storm. The morning sun hung suspended above the placid South Pacific waters, a bright yellow ball still low enough to spread dawn's hues of orange and pink throughout the vast oceanic sky.

As he lowered the binoculars, he caught a brief glimpse of something on the sand, something he had missed in his early morning travels on the beach.

He picked up a chunk of mango from his breakfast plate and popped it into his mouth, savoring the sweet, cold fruit while he pondered this new thing that had come to rest on his beach. Arms, legs, head . . . a human. A rather limp one.

He set the binocs down on his tray and sipped his coffee.

He supposed he would have to investigate further. There was no one else to whom he could delegate that task. The lack of "helper humans" on his island demonstrated that people weren't on his favorite species list. His island was fully automated, and his bots performed their tasks well, but he didn't own a bot capable of retrieving a human from the beach.

Troy reluctantly left his deck to get his tablet and drone. He sent the drone down to the beach, where it took video and basic vitals.

The human flotsam proved to be a young man, about 30 years of age, long-limbed, tan, shaggy sun-bleached hair. The drone registered his heartbeat as well as his breathing.

Damn! The fact that the castaway was still alive meant that Troy would now have to deal with him. He briefly thought about leaving him on the beach until he got up and found the house on his own, or until tropical storm Rae had her way with him. He pushed the thought away. Karma was a coldhearted bitch, as he well knew;

it wouldn't do to rack up bad karma. It shouldn't matter to him now, as old as he was, but for some reason, it did.

He took the elevator down and drove the buggy out to the boardwalk. He knew that if the flotsam had any serious injuries, it would be screwed, because Troy didn't have any means to convey the castaway safely back to the house without a lot of shifting and moving his body around. All Troy could do was bend at the waist and haul the body into the buggy by the arms and by the back of the shirt.

It took about ten minutes to get the lanky body haphazardly into the buggy so that it wouldn't slide out again on the fifty-yard drive back to the house. Troy had plenty of upper body strength to go around, and handling the castaway's body was like handling that of a really big fish – except that he had never handled a 6-foot, 190-pound fish before, and he'd always had a line to reel in.

He sat and rested for a few moments after dragging the body into the buggy. He tried to reach and rub the sharp new knot in the middle of his back. As he did, he looked over and studied the intruder's face.

He hadn't gotten a good look at the younger man during his earlier exertions. Now, Troy felt a sense of déjà vu at the sight of the broad, tanned face and snub nose.

He shook the feeling off. The stranger was too young for him to know or to have known during his previous life in the States.

At the top of the elevator, he maneuvered the dead weight into one of his extra chairs and used his remote to guide it into his "guest" room, where, once again, Troy was faced with heavy lifting. Cursing and muttering under his breath, he managed to get the torso, then legs, entirely onto the guest bed.

The space between Troy's shoulder blades complained sharply, and he knew his back would have its revenge on him by morning. He'd be lucky if he didn't end up lying flat in his bed for a week from the abuse he was heaping on his body . . . or at least, what was left of it.

He clumsily stripped off the stranger's sodden clothing, which were worn threadbare and bleached nearly transparent from days spent in salt water and exposure to the relentless Pacific sun.

He didn't bother trying to dress the castaway. He just left some of his largest, oldest shorts and a t-shirt at the foot of the bed.

Troy checked his vitals again using the MedScan, which provided a clearer analysis of his conditions than the drone had. Vitals were steady. No broken bones, but some deep contusions and a goose egg on the noggin. The worse diagnoses were exposure and dehydration.

Troy could handle cuts, bruises, and the sunburn, but sent for the MedBot to administer the IV. Despite being a hunk of metal and wires, the MedBot was surprisingly competent and gentle.

The reluctant host left the curtains closed and exited the dark room. It could be hours or even days before the intruder regained consciousness.

He wasn't about to take either of his boats out or send for medical help from the mainland, which was at least a couple of days away. According to the weather reports, the storm would hit within twenty-four hours, and he was fully equipped to take care of his uninvited guest for a week, if need be.

On his way to throw the tattered shorts and shirt into the trash bin, he noticed the wallet in the shorts pocket. Surprised, he said. "How the hell did he not lose *this*?"

He attempted to pull some identification out of the wallet, but everything was wet and stuck together. One of the limp cards tore a little when he tried to peel them apart.

"Nope."

He tossed the wallet, contents and all, into the dryer.

He glanced at the clock in the living room as he rolled through. "Damn!" he uttered.

The morning was nearly gone, and he was starving. All of the exertion of the last couple of hours had burned up what little fuel he had gained from his half-eaten breakfast.

One of the pastimes that he truly enjoyed and didn't use bots for was preparing food. He was too hungry to do a from-scratch lunch today, though, so he just heated his leftovers from the evening before and grabbed himself an imported brew. Smiling to himself beneath his overgrown, unruly moustache and beard, he said with a chuckle, "*Everything* here is imported. I'm in the middle of nowhere!"

He snapped his tray to his chair and returned to his favorite spot on the deck.

He popped the top on his beer bottle. He held the bottle up so that the early afternoon sunlight shone through the amber liquid.

"To you," he said, toasting the horizon.

In the seventeen years he'd lived on the island, he'd experienced the wrath of five tropical storms: one in 2039, two in 2041, one in 2044, and one in 2046. He supposed he'd been lucky to not to have been hit more often. But then, maybe his island was easy to miss, just the size of a pinpoint in the vast Pacific, and not even charted.

He finished his lunch and rolled into the kitchen to clean up his dishes. He looked in on his uninvited guest, even though there was no need. If anything changed, his cell phone would beep, but he had to satisfy his curiosity.

The human flotsam slept soundly, breathing easily. He hadn't changed position. Troy was almost disappointed. Though people weren't his strong suit, it had been months since he'd last had company.

He snapped his fingers, suddenly remembering. "Wallet!"

He pulled it out of the dryer and took it to the living room. He clicked on the satellite television, tuned it to the Weather Channel, and set himself to examining the contents of his guest's wallet.

"Hmm . . . coupla shopping discount cards . . . sixty-seven dollars . . . library card . . . destroyed photograph . . . aha! Driver's license!" He held the item up in front of him as though he had won a prize.

"Thomas Quinn. Age 33. Six-foot-one. Blue eyes. Blonde hair. Atlanta, Georgia."

Troy's forehead wrinkled as he concentrated, waving the driver's license to and fro as though fanning himself. "Thomas Quinn. Thomas Quinn . . . Tom Quinn . . . Tommy Quinn . . . *Tommy Quinn*."

His eyes widened and he felt the blood drain from his face as realization struck him. "No. It can't be!" He picked up his glasses from their place on his tray and examined the photo, which had been protected from the salt water by its lamination. "Oh, shit."

Because it *was*. "How the hell . . ."

He wasted no time. He rolled to the panic room behind the kitchen. He keyed the combination into the number pad beside the door, which clicked open to allow him admittance. He rolled inside, grabbed a cardboard box and set it on his tray. Rolling around the house, he removed various scattered paintings and framed photographs from his walls, and a collection of books from his shelf. He had hung the paintings himself, so they were within easy reach. Not everything fit in the box, so he stacked some of the paintings on top of the rest of its contents. Back in the panic room, he leaned the excess paintings and photographs on the floor, facing the wall. He set the box heavily on the floor. As he reversed from the room, he locked the door and closed it firmly behind him.

"That should do it," he said.

His phone alarm beeped.

* * *

Tommy blinked blearily, trying to focus on anything within his dim surroundings. A sharp, pulsing pain threatened to explode out of his forehead. His mouth tasted like dust, and his lips were excruciatingly chapped. He was conscious of his battered body: he felt like one big, aching bruise.

He found that he could move his arms and legs with a little effort, but sharp pains and stiffness convinced him to wait a while before trying to move a second time. He discovered that his left arm was attached to an IV drip whose bag hung suspended from a portable metal pole. But he could tell, even in the darkness, that he was not in a hospital room.

It didn't matter. He was in a comfortable bed, with a roof over his head, and he was dry. And most importantly, the bed was fixed in one spot: it didn't roll and sway relentlessly.

There was a whirring sound like a small toy car that had been wound up and let go. A robot rolled up to the bedside, red lights blinking from what Tommy took to be its "face". A female computerized voice emanated from speaker holes located on its "chin".

"Please relax, lay back, and rest. You are being treated for dehydration and exposure. Intervenes fluids are being administered. Please do not move unnecessarily or remove the needle from your arm."

Feeling slightly weirded out but comforted, all the same, Tommy did as the robot instructed and lay back against the pillows.

Just then, the door of the room swung open, flooding the dark room with sunlight. Tommy blinked and squinted against the sudden glare as a man seated in a wheelchair rolled into the room accompanied by a sour, nasty smell. He couldn't see the man's face; silhouetted as it was against the brightly lit doorway.

A bedside lamp clicked on.

When his eyes had adjusted, Troy saw the man sitting silently, contemplating him out of small, round, brown eyes. Wild gray unkempt hair stuck out every which way from the top of the man's head. It matched the gray, wiry hair that started at his chin and spread across his cheeks and down his neck.

He wore an oversized grayish-white t-shirt and an equally large pair of shorts. His arms and shoulders were sinewy and well-muscled. From his shorts, gaunt legs protruded awkwardly, as though they didn't know what position they were supposed to take. The skin on his legs hung loosely from his bones. His feet were bare.

Attached to the arms of the man's wheelchair was a shiny metal tray, upon which sat a glass of water, a medicine cup, and Tommy's wallet.

The old man cleared his throat. "Thomas Quinn," he said in a frail, scratchy voice. He picked up Tommy's wallet from his tray and set it on the bedside table. "I didn't take anything. I just wanted to know who I picked up off my beach. I dried it for you in the dryer. How are you feeling?"

Tommy open his parched mouth and croaked in a slow Southern United States drawl, "Awful. My head." He winced. Even talking hurt.

"Sorry. I didn't want Shelley to treat you for pain if you didn't have any. But I brought you water and some ibuprofen, just in case. Can you swallow?"

"I don't know."

"Well, here. Open. I can't help you sit up or prop you up, but I can hold the glass."

Tommy obliged, groaning as he tried to tip his head up just enough to where he could receive some water. He opened his mouth. The old man dropped the tablets in one at a time, each one followed by a tipping of the glass of water to Tommy's lips. He managed to choke them all down. The gagging wasn't caused so much by the tablets as by the old man's sour stench. Still, he tried to chug as much of the water as he could. The cold freshness was like heaven on his tongue.

"Not too much, just yet," Troy cautioned, pulling the glass away. "You'll get sick. But I'll bring you some soup and crackers in a little while." He pushed a button on the arm of his wheelchair, which reversed through the doorway. "You need to rest. Don't be afraid of Shelley, she's just a MedBot." He turned the chair to away from the room, then looked back over his shoulder. "The name's Steve." With that, he rolled away, the motorized chair making a high-pitched whining noise.

Tommy then realized that the relentless ache in his stomach was the sharp ache of hunger, made a little sharper by the few gulps of water he'd just taken. He couldn't remember how long ago his last meal had been. Days? A week? Two?

He knew that four ibuprofen on a completely empty stomach would likely make the hunger worse, if not make him sick. He hoped the old man would bring food soon.

* * *

As he rolled around the kitchen, Troy caught the weather report. He had designed an open floor plan to accommodate his chair, so he could easily see his widescreen in the living room. He watched the dark gray representation of the approaching storm: a huge cloudy cartoon-like whirlpool coiled in the South Pacific Ocean. It seemed so huge and so close to the island that it was incomprehensible to him that it hadn't made landfall yet. Looking past the television through his open French doors, all was still sunny and peaceful.

His thoughts turned to finding a way to get Tommy Quinn off of his island, but the reality of it was that they were going to sit tight while the storm blew through. If he tried to get Tommy to the mainland, he would run the risk of getting caught in the storm and killing them both. Both of his boats, *Melody* and *Harmony*, were already battened down inside the reinforced boathouse. The house would be sealed and ready for the storm with just a touch of a few buttons on his universal remote control.

Troy was just going to keep his fingers crossed that Tommy wouldn't guess his true identity. Troy disliked confrontation, and there was no telling how Tommy might react if he learned the truth. He didn't know how much Tommy knew or remembered about the past, but he was willing to guess that, if Tommy knew anything at all, the knowledge would not be to Troy's benefit.

At least here on the island, Troy had the security of knowing his own home and its nooks and crannies, as well as the island's geography. He had his Colt .47 if things got nasty. He'd bought the beautifully maintained antique gun mostly for show, but it would fire like new if he needed it to. And he could always retreat to his panic room.

The thought of his Colt prompted Troy to unlock the glass cabinet where he kept the firearm on display. It wouldn't hurt to load it and keep it with him – just in case his uninvited guest should prove to be hostile.

After loading it, he tucked the gun into the side pocket of his chair and took the castaway his lunch. Typical fare for someone who was ill: chicken soup made from last night's spit-roasted chicken, crackers, and green gelatin. Nothing heavy for a half-starved man.

Troy propped Tommy's pillows behind him, and Tommy pulled himself up into a sitting position. He was grateful for the food and thanked Troy profusely.

"Just take it easy," Troy responded. "Don't eat too fast."

He left Tommy to his meal. Having seen the younger man wrinkle his nose when Troy came near, Troy decided to go and bathe. There was never any real reason to practice good hygiene. Who was Troy going to offend? Millie, his cat?

Fresh from his bath, he checked on the castaway. The food was eaten, the flotsam, napping. Troy quietly took the dishes away.

Back on the deck, Troy lifted his binoculars. Was he seeing things, or did the horizon line look a little darker? Was the haze a little closer?

The sun had traversed its arc and now hung behind Troy's house, which cast a brief shadow down the front boardwalk. The quality of the light had changed. The sky's pastel blue had deepened, and the water's shade had become inscrutably dark.

The tide was beginning to turn. Waves lapped gently at the shore. Nothing seemed amiss, but Troy felt a distinct sense of unease. He scanned the water to the right and left along the beach as far as the view allowed. He decided to go for an outing.

He left his uninvited guest sleeping and took the elevator down. He drove the buggy off the boardwalk and south along the beach's edge. He used his binoculars often. He did the same on the way back, passing in front of the house and the edge of the boardwalk.

The ocean was calm, and Troy saw nothing out of the ordinary.

He returned to the house and sent his drone out from the deck. He sent it around the island as far as it could travel. The entire island seemed peaceful. The drone detected no intruders, and nothing unusual seemed to be happening that merited attention.

He took video of the ocean from the opposite side of the island. There, though the sky was still clear, the yellow ball was well into its slow descent toward the water. It was the perfect image of an idyllic sunset on a hidden tropical retreat.

The video taken from this side of the island was a little different.

Troy knew tropical storm Rae was coming in from the west. From where he sat, all he could see with his binoculars was that the dividing line between sea and sky was growing ever more hazy and dark. The drone recorded video of several large shapes approaching beneath the waters. They were too far away to determine what manner of fish they were. Troy surmised that they were a school of bottlenose dolphins.

"Hey, Steve. What's that?" Troy started at the sudden raspy Southern lilt behind him.

He moved his chair a little to the side so that he could see Tommy propped up against the door frame.

"Hi Thomas," Troy said. "Where's the IV? Shelley should scan your vitals before you move around."

Tommy flapped a hand. "Call me Tommy, and she already did. She told me to take it easy and to drink lots of water, but she took out the IV." He rubbed his arm where a piece of gauze was taped to it. "Still getting used to not bobbing around like a cork in the middle of the ocean."

"You can sit down." Troy nodded toward a grouping of outdoor furniture arranged at the corner of the deck.

"Thanks." Tommy walked uncertainly to the grouping and slowly dragged a lounge chair close to where Troy sat. “This is a pretty sweet spot. Where are we, exactly?”

“I can’t tell you, *exactly*. But I can give you a guess. Somewhere in the South Pacific between South America and Australia.”

“Thank you for your hospitality. Y’all probably saved my life.”

Troy shrugged and said nothing.

The silence stretched on.

“So . . . what were y’all looking at?”

Troy looked up from his tablet. “There’s supposed to be a tropical storm coming in, but all I can see is a big wall of haze.”

“And there’s something in the water?”

“Probably just dolphins.”

“Are we safe to be in a storm? Is there anyone else here?”

“Oh yeah, we’re safe. I’ve already been through a few storms out here. Learned the hard way how to keep my house from blowing away. And myself.” He chuckled. “Yes, there are a few of other people around,” he lied vaguely, “But I like to spend time alone.”

A marmalade cat strolled casually out onto the deck. Troy moved his tablet just in time, clearing his lap for the cat’s landing there. “In case you haven’t met her yet, this is Millicent Oberon McGillicutty. Millie, for short.” He petted the cat, mouthing baby talk.

Tommy watched the old man pet the marmalade cat. “So . . . what are the chances of getting home from here?”

“I can get you close enough to the States to get you home, but not until after the storm blows over. Don’t worry, though. I’ve got satellite TV and internet. If you like to read, I have a nice little library. You’ll be comfortable enough for another day or two. You should be resting, anyway. Hey, by the way, where did you come from? How did you get here from . . . Georgia, was it? How did you make it halfway around the world from there?"

It was Tommy's turn to shrug. "I actually didn't come from Georgia to here. I was visiting friends in Cali . . . went for a boat ride and got caught in a freak storm. Got knocked out, landed on a big piece of boat. Floated around awhile. And here I am."

Troy scrutinized Tommy's face for a moment. "Hm. You're looking a little pale under your tan. I think you got out of bed too soon. Feel free to use the sofa if you don't feel like going back to bed."

"Y'all may be right." Tommy rose carefully from his chair and slowly made his way inside.

"I'll get dinner together in a little while," Troy called after him.

* * *

Tommy closed the bedroom door behind him and sat heavily on the bed. Shelley buzzed over to him.

"You need to rest," she said. "Drink more water."

Obeying, Tommy picked up the glass that the old man had left on the bedside table earlier and took a few sips of the water. He noticed a drawer in the bedside table and, curious, slid it open. It contained only a framed photograph. He pulled it from the drawer.

The photo was of a man in his forties; short dark hair, a smile that reached the corners of his eyes. Tommy knew this man immediately. He hadn't recognized his elderly host, with his matted beard and crazy Einsteinian tufts of gray hair; but he knew him, now. And his name wasn't Steve. It was Troy Fairchild.

The very man Tommy had been searching for.

* * *

Millie yowled in complaint.

Troy stroked her back. "Just a few minutes, Miss McGillicutty," he said. She yowled in response, her paw striking out, her claws extended for slashing.

"Hey!" Troy exclaimed. Millie jumped down and paced the deck, her tail swaying slowly from side to side. She stopped every few minutes to groom herself and yowl.

"Who pissed in your cornflakes?" He asked her. She ignored him.

The same three geckos had been sunning themselves on the deck since early that morning. It was about the time of day when they retreated to hot, sunbaked rocks for the night; except they were retreating in the wrong direction. Troy watched the three of them climb up the side of the house to the roof.

All of the remaining geckos on the island (or so it seemed to Troy) suddenly poured over the edge of the deck in droves. Troy sat in stunned surprise for a split second, then quickly reversed his chair through the French doors and hit the "Close Door" button on his universal house remote. The doors swung shut even as the swarm of geckos reached the threshold. It seemed they were seeking higher ground: they followed the first three up the front wall of the house. Troy watched their little toes and tails flatten against the glass as they scurried up the outer surface of the French doors.

At first, when the flood of geckos tapered off and his windows cleared, Troy thought the storm had finally arrived and that the high winds were sending pieces of vegetation and tree branches swirling about in the air. After a moment, however, he discovered that what he actually saw and heard through the three-inch thick shatterproof glass was the flight of birds. Hundreds upon hundreds of birds, mostly parrots, though there were several flaming orange doves among their number, as well as a surprising few "golden-maned" hornbills, huge against the more petite members of their company.

It was normal for the island wildlife to act out of character before a bout of extreme weather conditions, and this wasn't the first time he had seen this behavior from his fellow island dwellers. Still, what appeared to be an exodus to higher ground nonplussed him enough that he spent some time in his communications room, listening to NWR for any updated information about the approaching storm. There was nothing new; only the repeated admonition that the storm would make landfall within the next twenty-four hours and the usual warnings about evacuation or storm preparation.

He returned to his living room to find the castaway reclining in the corner of his sofa, long legs stretched out before him.

"Feeling better?" Troy asked.

"A little." Tommy drawled vaguely, looking preoccupied.

"You hungry?"

Tommy's sharp blue eyes focused on Troy a little more clearly. "Shore am. That soup y'all brought me before was awesome, but something solid would help, now."

The old man nodded and stowed his binoculars on a shelf, then removed the tray from his chair. After setting it aside, he rummaged in the refrigerator and pulled out two of the swordfish steaks he had stored that morning, as well as the prawns. He was going to use the indoor grill.

"Storm getting closer." Tommy called to him.

"Yeah," Troy responded, gathering his ingredients. "It's getting rough outside." He turned on his grill to heat, and prepared a marinade of fresh coconut milk, ginger, and lime juice. He threw some green chile and jalapeño peppers into his food processor for a few seconds and added them to the marinade. Troy dropped the prawns into the marinade and popped the bowl back into the refrigerator.

Tommy got up from the sofa and joined Troy in the kitchen. "Mind if I get more water?" he asked.

"Help yourself."

Tommy filled his glass with ice from the icemaker in the refrigerator door, then with water from the dispenser. He took a seat at the table and watched Troy drop the swordfish steaks on the hot grill. "Y'all's pretty good with those wheels," he commented.

Troy glanced at him briefly. "I've been in them a few years. Long enough to learn how to work them."

"So . . . what happened? If y'all don't mind me asking."

"Car accident."

"A collision?"

"You could say that . . ." Troy tossed mango and papaya chunks with freshly shaved coconut. "A car collided with me while I was strolling down a sidewalk one day."

"Damn, that sucks, man. Did they catch the guy?"

Troy didn't look at him as he dropped his marinated prawns into a hot frying pan. "Yeah, they caught the guy." He brandished a pair of wine glasses. "White wine?"

"Shore! Why not? So it wasn't hit and run?"

"Oh yeah, it was a hit and run. But they found the driver." Troy flipped the swordfish steaks and checked the prawns, then rolled back and forth through the kitchen, setting plates, silverware, fruit, and bread on the table. He checked the seafood again. "I believe we're in business."

"Awesome! Smells amazing."

"We'll see." He plated the steaks and prawns.

They dug in.

After a few minutes, Tommy broke the silence. "I wonder if this storm is the same one that I got caught in."

"Doubtful. If you were off the California coast, you would have been too far north. This tropical storm originated more to the south."

"Hm." Tommy sipped his wine.

"So what do you do, Tommy?"

"Me? Oh, I design warm weather sportswear. For skaters, surfers, you know. Board shorts, shoes, t-shirts, jerseys."

Troy raised his eyebrows. "Really. That's interesting."

"And how about y'all, Steve? How did you get yourself this little island?

"Settlement."

"Ah. Say no more."

"Shall we adjourn to the Weather Channel?"

Tommy scraped his chair back and reclaimed his seat in one corner of the sofa. "Wow," he said. "Looks like a total doozy."

After clearing the table, Troy hit the kitchen light switch on the way into the living room, leaving the television as the only source of light. He stared out the doors at the approaching fog bank, which had reached the island. The glare of the floodlights now cast the swirling, roiling mass in an eerie greenish tint. It looked like something from an experimental science class beaker. He looked up, but the fog seemed to continue up toward the sky without end. It continued on into the blackness to the right and left, beyond the reach of the floodlights. He guessed that even if he could identify the line between light and dark, he still wouldn't be able to see where the fog bank ended – in either direction. It advanced inland at a slow crawl, like a sluggish, mindless animal.

"You look nervous. I thought y'all said you've been through a few storms out here."

Troy turned his head and gave him a brief glance. "I have. But I've never seen anything like that since I've lived here."

"That's not normal?"

Troy reflected for a moment. "There *is* fog, sometimes. It just doesn't usually look like *that*." He thought about the images of the dark shapes beneath the water that his drone had captured. Was he sure they were dolphins?

At that moment, the two men heard a scream from the direction of the beach.

"What the hell is *that*?" Tommy asked, a note of alarm in his voice. He clamped his hands to his ears as more screams erupted from the beach, rising in pitch and volume, creating an intolerable din.

Troy looked past him, down to the shore.

As he watched, something emerged from the roiling edges of the fog. Its lumbering movements reminded Troy of a giant sea lion. Was it an elephant seal, maybe a walrus? Whatever it was used long front flippers to propel itself along the sand.

But its head looked human.

More of the things came out of the fog and lumbered up the beach toward Troy's house. He recalled the video feed the drone had sent to his tablet earlier. The dark shadows swimming below the surface of the ocean, ahead of the wall of haze.

A sudden stench assailed his nostrils. It permeated his walls and filled his living room and kitchen: the rotting, revolting smell of decomposing fish.

"What *are* those things? What the hell is that smell? Hey, where y'all going?"

But Troy had rolled away. He reappeared in a few seconds with his drone.

He didn't like opening his doors after he had already sealed up the house and enabled his fortifications against the impending tropical storm, but he only needed to open them enough to launch the drone.

It flew over the creatures on the beach, feeding video back to Troy's tablet. His stomach dropped with fear as he observed the images.

The creatures' front arms were flipper-esque, ending in webbed claws. They had no rear legs, just massive, scale-covered tails which they dragged behind them as they approached. From the waist up, the creatures' oversized chests seemed to be covered in a thick, coarse fur, resembling that of a sea lion. The fur continued up their necks, where it tapered off below the chin. Their faces were smooth, black, and vaguely humanoid, but where a human nose would have been was a bump containing two vertical slits. A thick black ridge jutted out above golden eyes that glowed, fish-like, in the floodlights' glare. Their black pupils were also vertical slits, similar to how a cat's pupils looked in bright light. Hair grew from the rough heads, long and dripping with seaweed, or maybe algae, and hung down their backs. Dark slashes that resembled gills appeared on either side of their necks.

Tommy looked over Troy's shoulder. "Holy shit, those things are fugly!"

The older man had to agree. The things *were* fugly. They were strange, abnormal. Like really nastyass mermaids – or mer*men* – but were they a threat?

Just then, one of them tipped its head back, opened its mouth and screamed, revealing triple rows of razor sharp teeth. The other creatures followed suit, screaming in answer. The result was a shrill cacophony, a sound more *felt* than heard, that reverberated sharply through the men's heads. Tommy dropped to his knees, clutching his ears. Troy recoiled against the back of his chair.

If he'd had doubts before, the old man had none, now. These things *were* a threat, even if it came only in the form of a sound that could bloody his eardrums. Those teeth might be something to be concerned about, too. He hoped the main diet of these mermonsters was fish and other seafood. He thought wryly that perhaps they had smelled his dinner.

He grabbed his flashlight from the bookshelf, hustled to the bathroom and pulled two pairs of earplugs from the box he kept in his medicine cabinet. Experience had taught him that tropical storms could be tremendously loud. He had prepared accordingly and stocked up on earplugs. Maybe they would help against the creatures' shrill screams. For good measure, he also grabbed two headsets from his communications room.

He rolled out to the living room and tossed a pair of each at Tommy, who was pale and visibly shaken. "They can't get in here, can they?" he asked nervously.

Troy jammed earplugs in his ears and put his headset on. "I don't think so. The only access from the first floor is through a three-inch thick stainless steel elevator door, which is on lock-down for the storm, and a hidden trapdoor under two feet of sand. Unless they can somehow climb up the outside of the building, they shouldn't even be able to reach the second floor."

"Let's hope they don't have suction cups on those flippers. What if they *do* somehow reach the second floor?"

The old man shuddered at the image. "Those French doors would be the one spot I would worry about," he said. "But that's shatter-resistant glass, and I had state-of-the-art electronic slide bolts installed; there are sixteen of them, from top to bottom. The door frame isn't even wood, though it looks like wood that's been painted white. It's white-painted stainless steel. And they are sealed through air pressure. There are several other windows up here, but they all use shatter-resistant glass and the same electronic slide bolts, and they're sealed, too. Again, the only way to get to any of the second floor openings is by ladder . . . or by somehow climbing up the side of the building. And even if those things could climb, they wouldn't be able to get inside the glass. They wouldn't be able to break it. I'm not an expert on sea monsters, but I'm not sure those things can climb."

"I feel a lot better," Tommy responded.

A piercing shriek rose from the beach, followed by an ear-splitting answering chorus. Tommy quickly stuffed the ear plugs into his ears and added the headset.

Troy said, "I want to try to figure out why they're here. What do they want?"

"I don't know, but that fog is getting closer."

In the dimness, Tommy watched the sea creatures flop their way up the beach, the fog bank close behind them, their tails being chased by ocean water. *Water*?

"Steve?" he said, "Didn't the tide already come in? Weren't we at high tide over an hour ago?"

"Why?" Troy joined him at the edge of the French doors.

"Because it looks like the tide is still coming in." Tommy pointed to the gently lapping water's edge, which had advanced up the beach just beneath the fog bank.

Troy rubbed his hairy chin, his brow furrowed. "I don't understand. That water is almost all the way up to the house."

"Is the island sinking?"

"I don't know."

"Is your house waterproof?"

"Supposed to be."

Tommy felt frustration building throughout his chest at the old man's noncommittal answers. He wasn't promising safety. Therefore, there was a chance that his reinforced walls would *not* hold back the pressure of the entire South Pacific.

The two men stared silently from the dark interior of Troy's house at the mermonsters, the sickly green-tinted fog bank and the rising ocean water.

Should have stayed in bed this morning, Troy thought. He had rarely feared anything in his life. The few things that had inspired fear in him were when he'd first lost the use of his legs, and he was wondering how he was going to take care of himself for the rest of his life. Other moments in which he had felt fear were during the previous tropical storms he'd experienced. Aside from that, for the past several years, he'd had nothing to fear on his isolated island. It was only him, the lizards, and scads of exotic birds, not to mention some delicious ocean fish. The millipedes could be annoying, but the most he had to fear from them was a painful bite – as long as it was above the waist. Below the belt down to his toes, they could bite all they wanted and he wouldn't feel a thing.

He had seen some strange weather phenomena and the occasional unusual flora or fauna during his years as the island's only human inhabitant. Until tonight, however, he'd had yet to witness any kind of intimidating or deadly wildlife. He could safely say that the mermonsters scared the shit out of him, and he wasn't afraid to admit it, but he kept it to himself, anyway. He was still questioning that he was even seeing the nightmarish creatures.

He found himself double-checking his fortifications in his head, reviewing the list of storm preparation plans that he had developed over the past decade.

Elevator locked and sealed. Check. Windows closed and sealed: kitchen, check. Living room, check. Bedroom, guestroom, check, check . . . he had sealed the windows in the bathroom, and the communications room. There were no windows in the panic room. The French doors were closed, locked, and sealed. Two backup generators at the ready: check. Dry goods and canned supplies, bottled water: check. Sterno: check.

"I think I know what those things are," Tommy said, sounding hesitant.

Troy eyed the younger man with a wary look. "Yeah? What?"

"Have y'all ever heard of sirens?"

Troy was silent for a moment, waiting for the translator inside his head to catch up. "You talking about the myth? Those mermaid things that hang out on treacherous rocks and lead sailors astray with their unearthly singing? You gotta be kidding. These things sound as hideous as they look."

"What if the myths, or legends, or whatever they are – what if they just got – you know – modified, as time went on? Romanticized?" He snorted a brief laugh and went on nervously, "What if the macho sailors didn't want to admit that they'd been bested by a bunch of fugly mermaid men, so they made up stories about the things having these beautiful singing voices that entranced them into foundering on the rocks? I mean, a *siren* is really one of the worst noises in the world."

"What the hell? Sounds like you're just talking to make yourself feel better."

"So maybe I am," Tommy said weakly, and lapsed into silence.

Troy felt a moment of pity for his unwanted guest, who was surely wishing he was anywhere else right now, regardless of his motivations for being here – if, indeed, he had any. Could Lily Mercy's stepson really have washed up on Troy's beach by accident?

"Is there anything else we can do to get through this? Safely, I mean?" Tommy tried to make up for his earlier faux pas.

"No. I think all that we can do is treat this the same as any severe tropical storm." The old man looked Tommy in the eye. "We wait it out."

Tommy stared out at the fog, which had begun to shroud the house. He could barely see the dark water, and couldn't tell whether it had reached the house's foundation, because the deck blocked his view.

He pulled up one of Troy's comfortable arm chairs and found a position just inside of the French door to the left.

The mermonsters seemed an aggressive and foul-tempered species. They lunged and snapped at the others when they came too close, and their interactions seemed to consist mainly of fighting amongst each other. Periodically, the creatures' voices would all rise together in a scream, always in answer to one who screamed first. The noise still emitted a painful frequency, but the ear plugs muffled the noise just enough to dull its debilitating effects.

The water had risen about six feet – enough for them to swim.

"You know," said Troy, echoing Tommy's thoughts, "If the water keeps rising, they'll be able to swim onto the deck."

Tommy suddenly stood and stretched. He walked into the kitchen and grabbed a beer from the fridge.

"Help yourself," Troy said, watching.

"Don't mind if I do," Tommy shot back. He twisted off the cap, took a long guzzle. "What else is there to do? What would y'all have done if this had been the storm y'all expected?"

"Probably would have sat and waited. Definitely wouldn't be drinking too much, just in case something happened."

"Like weird and scary sea monsters swimming out of the mysterious fog?"

"Yeah, I guess that counts as something happening."

"Do y'all have any way of defending yourself at all? What if pirates landed here and found your house?"

"They wouldn't find anything worth taking," Troy said.

"Are y'all kidding? All of y'all robots and electronic whatsis? Not to mention a room full of all that art? *Troy*?"

"Excuse me?"

Tommy took a long slug of his beer. "Come on, your name isn't 'Steve'. I know y'all Troy Fairchild. You're the guy that put my Mama away for attempted murder."

"I don't know what you're talking about," Troy said, as he thought, *oh, shit*.

"Don't lie, old man. I found your stupid picture in the bedside table draw. And when I saw the blank squares on the wall, the big empty spot on your bookshelf with all the dust around it . . . I figured y'all hid my Mama's things so I wouldn't find out who y'all were. That don't matter, anyway, I've known y'all were here for a couple of years. This just isn't how I planned it. My boat wrecked, leaving me floating for who knows how long." He gestured with his beer bottle toward the French doors. "And now, those things, you know."

"Damn, I *knew* it was too weird to be coincidence. You're choosing *right now* to air your grievances? Has it occurred to you that your timing is off? Don't you think you should have said something earlier? Perhaps as dinner conversation? And you *planned* this?"

"I thought I had more time! Then those *things* showed up – and I have a really bad feeling that we haven't seen they true ugliness yet – butI needed to say something before it gets worse. Y'all hurt my Mama, and y'all had her put away, and y'all took her *away* from me!" Tommy's face was red with fury. "And if *those* things don't kill y'all tonight, I *will*!"

"Thomas, your mother hit me with her *car*! She crippled me for life, almost killed me! Yes, I had her put away!"

"Y'all got the wrong lady! And even if it *was* her, who would blame her, after everything y'all did to her. You crazy old loser, you creepy old *stalker*! Y'all drove her crazy and ruined her life, and she killed herself in prison because of you! *Y'all killed her*!"

"*She did it to herself*!" Troy yelled at him. He surreptitiously reached down into the side pocket of his chair, feeling the heavy comfort of his Colt .47. "And you'd better watch it, or I'll send you out to meet your – your *sirens*!"

"Like y'all could, you stinking cripple!

"*Try me*." The old man looked at Tommy steadily, forcing Tommy to drop his eyes to the floor. "*Your mother was disturbed. She hit me. With.* Her *car*. And she wasn't even your real mom. She was your *step*mother."

"She *was* my real Mama! She loved me as her own son. Y'all stalked her and drove her *insane*! It's fitting that y'all can't walk anymore. The punishment fits the crime! But my Mama committed no crime! Y'all got the wrong damned *lady*."

Troy thought back. He remembered hearing about Lily's suicide like it happened yesterday . . . and relived the guilt he had felt when he had learned that Lily had left a great portion of her estate to him. He had wondered for a long time why she would try to kill him when she had left him money, many of her paintings, first edition signed copies of her books . . . and had the royalties for their sales transferred to him upon her death. If she were going to try to kill him, why would she not have changed her will?

He recalled the summer day as he was walking downtown in Ann Arbor, Michigan. It was Lily's car. He knew that, for sure: a cool blue Buick four-door sedan with her signature fox animal ornament dangling from the rear-view. The vehicle bore down on him and jumped the sidewalk. There was a sudden glare on the windshield from the bright afternoon sun, and he couldn't see the driver well. But only Lily ever drove Lily's car.

The car didn't stop. It swiped him as he turned to run, hitting him in the lower back. Then it kept going, just raced away down the empty street as he crumpled to the cement and lay there, helpless, beneath the summer Sunday sunshine.

He looked up at Tommy. Something about his face. His angry expression . . .

Red hot rage erupted suddenly from the pit of Troy's stomach and coursed upward, infusing his brain. "*You.* It was *you*! *You* tried to kill me! It wasn't her, at all!" His vision blurred as tears of anger and sadness filled his eyes. "You did it and let your mother take the fall. She killed herself out of shame for what you did!" A new realization dawned on him. "You knew, didn't you? You knew I was a beneficiary. You wanted what she left to me. You selfish, soulless little–"

"*No*!" Tommy advanced on Troy, towering over him, his fist raised.

Troy pulled the Colt .47 from the side pocket of his chair and held it in trembling, bony hands. He cocked it. "Because of you, I've been exiled to a life of misery. You destroyed the thread that made my life meaningful." He put his finger on the trigger. Then he noticed that Tommy had stopped dead, his fist still raised, his mouth hanging wide open. He kept aim on Tommy as he slowly turned his head.

Silence met him as he looked into the golden fish-eyes of the monster peering back at him through the French door. "Oh, shit," Troy said.

While the men had argued, the water level had risen rapidly. Their shouting had attracted the sea monsters. Three of them had simply floated with the water level – and now sat on Troy's deck.

Troy maneuvered his chair so that he was facing the door, and slowly reversed to a safer distance.

"Okay," Tommy said quietly. "So *that* happened. Still think they can't get in?"

Troy looked at the bottom of the French doors. There was easily two feet of water above the threshold, but so far it didn't look like one drop had breached the seal. His floor was dry. He cleared his throat. "I'm willing to think positive."

"Do y'all have any other defenses in this place – besides that gun? Like a Robocop knockoff or something? And those things must weigh a ton each. Why the hell hasn't your deck splintered?"

"Yeah. K9 bots. But they're kind of allergic to water. Never thought I would have to defend myself from a sea creature this high in the air. The deck has been fortified, just like the rest of my house. Plus the water is making them lighter . . . I don't know how that works."

"Just to let y'all know," Tommy hissed, "I'm not after my Mama's material possessions because I need her money. She left me comfortable, but I haven't had to live off of her legacy. I make a successful living doing what I do. I've come to take back the things of hers y'all took because y'all are slime and y'all don't deserve them, *and* to finish the job."

Troy held the eyes of the mermonster before him. He slowly raised his gun, still cocked, and aimed it steadily at the creature. "You did wrong, Tommy. You framed your mother. And you know that's the reason she's dead, now. And me? I never would have hurt her. I loved her. She loved me. Why would I do that?"

"Good question. Because you're sick?"

The mermonster on the deck opened its gaping maw. The triple rows of lethally sharp teeth glinted a dull yellow in the floodlights. *My entire head would fit inside that thing's mouth,* Troy thought.

The thing shrieked.

Its fellows shrieked in answer. The headphones and earplugs did very little to protect Troy's ears at this close range. The pitch rose shrilly, higher and higher until it passed out of comprehension and Troy was ready to pass out.

At first, he thought he pulled the trigger on his Colt .47, because a spot appeared in his shatter resistant glass. Then he found that he had lowered the weapon and it now rested safely in his lap.

He reversed his chair as more spots appeared in the glass. Cracks broke free from the spots and ran like spider webs across the glass, which then splintered and fell into the water that now poured into the room.

The biggest creature lunged, crashing through the bare frames of the French doors. The frames crumpled to the floor, taking the sixteen stainless steel sliding bolts with them.

It screamed again, and Troy smelled its rancid breath, felt the heat of it on his face. He thought his eardrums would burst.

"AAAaaaaaahhhhhhh!" Tommy screamed, his hands to his ears. He rushed toward Troy. "Take him! Take him!" He grabbed the handles on the back of Troy's chair and tried to push the old man toward the monsters, but Troy had his fingers on the "Reverse" button, fighting him. With his free hand, Troy cocked his gun again, and, aiming backward and upside down over his shoulder, he pulled the trigger. The kick from the discharge pushed Troy's arm up and forward, and he dropped the weapon. He hit the "Brake" button on his remote, but that was a mistake. The sudden stop combined with the gun's kick, as well as Tommy's shoving, made the chair flip forward, dumping Troy into the ocean water that flooded his floor.

He gasped at the sudden cold. He splashed around, trying to keep his head above the quickly rising water. He dragged himself on his elbows to his chair and attempted to push it upright. Desperate tears streamed down his face as he fumbled around, trying to get the chair to sit upright. He held himself up with one hand and wrangled the chair with the other until he somehow managed to push it at the correct angle, and it landed firmly on its wheels in the upright position.

He grabbed the armrests and started pulling himself up. As he did so, he glanced up and saw that he had missed his target. Tommy stood there, frozen in terror, staring into the face of the sea monster, who paid Troy no attention, but stared back at Tommy and screamed.

Troy redoubled his efforts. He had just maneuvered himself into his seat when the beast lunged.

Tommy screamed and threw his arms up protectively in front of his face. The monster grabbed at him with its claws.

Troy made for his panic room, rolling through the rising water. It was already halfway up his shins. "Millie!" he called, suddenly thinking of his foul-tempered feline. An orange blur launched itself from the kitchen counter onto his lap. "Ah, there you are, my little baby!"

Paying no heed to whatever was behind him, he punched in the combination to the panic room lock with shaking fingers. He slammed it behind him, locked and sealed it.

He had opened and closed the door quickly enough that not a lot of water had rushed in with him; still, he rolled around the room, picking Lily's paintings up off the floor, finding higher places upon which to set them: on top of extra shelves already bursting with old belongings, balancing them on top of overflowing boxes. He found high places for her books, as well.

Altogether, she had left him eleven paintings and nine books. She had shared the royalties for six of those books with him. He still received checks.

Soon, a loud pounding ensued upon the panic room door. Troy didn't care. If the monsters got him, they got him. He sat and gazed at his favorite painting. It was a painting of Lily and himself, together; her head on his chest, staring softly and sleepily at the artist. In the painting, Troy was wide awake. Lily had painted it from imagination, but it looked as though the painting could have been done from a photograph.

Tears ran unchecked down the old man's cheeks. "I'm so sorry, Lily . . . I didn't know." He sobbed until the pounding ceased and all was quiet. A faint breezed brushed his damp forehead in the windowless room.

He fell asleep in his sodden clothing, but it didn't matter. The room was like a sauna. Miss McGillicutty slept comfortably on his lap.

The panic room door, though marred with huge dents, had held firm.

When he woke, Troy rolled through his living room, squelching across his sodden throw rugs to assess the damage of another, different kind of storm.

Of Thomas Quinn, there was no sign. The ocean had receded to its proper place, and the monsters had gone.

The rising sun turned the page of another heavenly South Pacific morning.

THE LEAST OF US

"Mommy, Mommy, look what I found!"

Darce O'Neil turned from the sink she was filling with hot, soapy water for the dishes. "Chelsea! Where have you been? Look at you!" Grimy dirt covered Chelsea's face and clothes. Her blonde hair was gray with cobwebs.

"I was playing in the attic, Mommy. Look what I found!"

"Chelsea! You know you aren't supposed to be playing up there! It's dirty and dangerous. Who knows what – what is that?"

"It's a doll, Mommy! Look at her!"

Gingerly, Darce reached out and took the thing. It was, indeed, a doll. It wore a dingy bonnet and jumper that may have been white, once upon a time. Beneath the jumper were an equally dingy blue shirt and two or three layers of petticoats. A darkish- colored cloak covered the doll's shoulders and draped its back.

She brushed the dirt from the doll's face. Its facial features were unremarkable. Wide-set gray eyes, pale complexion, straight nose; thin lips, parted slightly.

Darce turned it upside down, looking for a tag or other marking that would indicate where it was made. She found nothing except grimy underskirts.

The doll seemed completely ordinary. Still, there was something about it that Darce didn't like.

"Can I keep her?"

"I don't know, Chelsea. She looks really old. And she's really, really dirty."

"But it'll wash off! I'll clean her up! We can wash her clothes, or I can make new ones. Can I keep her, please, please, please?"

Darce looked at Chelsea's upturned, pleading face. "Honey, you have lots of dolls –"

"But this one's different! She's special! Pleeeaaasse?"

Darce hesitated a moment longer. *Maybe it's just the dirt that makes it seem unappealing,* she thought.

She sighed. "Get her clothes off; I'll see what I can do with them. Wash her up with lots of soap and water."

"Oh, thank you, thank you, Mommy! I love you!"

Chelsea grabbed her mother around the waist and stretched to kiss her cheek. Darce bent down to receive Chelsea's kiss; then the little girl turned and skipped away.

"Whoa, whoa, young lady!" Darce called after her. "Run yourself the bath and just take her in with you! You're as dirty as she is!"

As she looked after her daughter, the doll's gray eyes caught hers.

She could have sworn it was looking right at her.

* * *

Chelsea adored Jane, but Darce couldn't help feeling an aversion to her. Whenever Jane was in the room with her, Darce felt that the doll was staring at her.

She tried to shrug it off. *Of course,* she thought, *it's just an optical illusion . . . the same way the eyes of people in photographs follow you, or the eyes of statues and figurines.*

Or maybe it was just a spin-off of childhood fears. She'd had shelves full of dolls as a child, and had always feared that they were watching her, so she had turned them all to face away from her at bedtime.

Still, at tuck-in time, when Darce leaned down to kiss Chelsea good night . . . she felt that Jane was somehow mocking her. In the car, she couldn't help but be acutely aware of the doll's presence beside her in the front seat.

* * *

Chelsea turned nine on a Saturday in August. She had a fairy-themed birthday party. Her little guests all showed up wearing fairy dresses, and Darce provided wings and wands.

The day was everything it should have been for a little girl's birthday. The grassy backyard was lush and brilliant green beneath the cloudless blue sky, from which the sun beamed down as though it had been specially ordered just for the day. Lunch and birthday cake were consumed, gifts were opened, and the girls played for hours.

As Chelsea's guests departed with their parents in the late afternoon, the sky began to fill with ominous dark clouds.

"That was really fun," Chelsea said.

"I'm glad you enjoyed yourself, and I hope your friends did, too," her mother replied.

"But now I'm tired."

"Too tired to play with your birthday gifts?"

"Yes."

"Why don't we go inside, watch a little television, and relax?"

"Okay," Chelsea agreed. She helped her mother gather her gifts and bring them inside. She skipped into the living room, her fairy wings fluttering gently against her back.

As a light rain began tapping on the roof, Darce turned on some lamps to dispel the deepening gloom. She tuned the television to Nickelodeon, and she and Chelsea snuggled together beneath the afghan on the sofa.

"Thank you for such a special birthday," Chelsea said drowsily, nestling beside her mother.

"You're very welcome, sweetheart."

Tired from the day's festivities and lulled by the steady sound of rain tapping on the eaves, Darce drifted into sleep, still wearing her baby blue satin fairy dress and fairy wings.

* * *

The booming sound of thunder woke her, followed by cartoon voices from the television.

She opened her eyes and saw Jane standing over her, smiling. But Jane wasn't a doll anymore. She was a real woman.

Darce's stomach dropped and terror clamped a fist around her heart. She tried to scream, but the sound caught in her throat, trapped behind closed, stiff, unmoving lips.

She struggled to move, but her arms and legs seemed paralyzed.

"Greetings, Darce O'Neil," Jane said. Her non-descript face had gained an angular harshness. Her soft eyes were now hard and cold, shining brightly in the dimness. Her thin lips twisted in a smirk. She leaned down and grabbed Darce around the waist, lifting her with massive hands. She carried Darce down the hall to the bathroom, where she turned on the light and held Darce up so that she faced the mirror.

Darce tried to scream again, but only silence issued forth from the motionless face reflected in the mirror.

"Why, Mrs. O'Neil, aren't you just the little doll?" Jane said, and laughed.

That's exactly what Darce was. A little doll, dressed in a baby blue satin dress. The shimmering fairy wings left over from Chelsea's birthday party poked out from behind her shoulders.

This is just a nightmare, Darce thought. *Just a nightmare that seems really real. I'll wake up any minute.*

"How appropriate," Jane said. "A little blue fairy doll. Who would ever suspect that there was anyone inside?" She rapped her knuckles roughly against the side of Darce's head. There was no pain; only a light sensation of contact.

"Oh, no, it doesn't hurt a bit! Isn't that nice? You won't feel anything but endless despair, wondering if you'll ever draw another human breath again. I know. I've been in that doll mold for about . . . eh, one hundred forty-eight years, give or take. Hmm."

Watching Jane's face in the mirror, Darce saw her eyes lose focus as she drifted into thought; then, just as quickly, Jane seemed to snap back to.

"Oh, so sorry! How remiss of me. I'm sure you would love to know who I am, and how I came to be here, and, more importantly, how *you* ended up in *your* current predicament."

She set Darce down on the bathroom counter and pulled the bonnet from her head, loosening long, thick silver waves.

"I was a powerful woman in my town. People feared me and my special abilities. But they couldn't kill me. They created a doll Vessel as a prison for me." She threw her head back and laughed: a low, deep laugh that sounded nothing like a woman. Her teeth were yellow, rotten, some broken. She picked up Darce's hairbrush from the bathroom counter and started brushing out her hair.

"They used my own power to chain me. Fools! They believed that I could never escape." She rolled her eyes and sighed. "So many years . . . sitting in the dark, in countless closets . . . mildewed basements . . . musty attics . . . but look at me now!" She spun around, smiling. "Ah, they used my own enchantment, one that I knew how to escape . . . difficult, but not impossible. And your daughter has been indispensable in helping me gain my freedom. Unwitting, of course. Oh, the innocent. Now, my worries are over. They have become *yours*."

A flood of fear rose steadily inside the well of Darce's stomach. *Chelsea!*

Jane tossed the brush on to the bathroom counter and picked Darce up. "Don't you worry about your little girl, Darce O'Neil," she said. "She will be well cared for. Especially since she may yet be of use to me. Oh, you didn't think she was going to stay with *you*?" She said, carrying Darce down the hall. "Obviously, *you* can't care for her in your current condition. And *someone* needs to take care of her."

Darce again made a fruitless effort to scream, to kick, to struggle.

As they passed through the living room, Darce could hear Chelsea's groggy voice.

"Jane, is that you? Oh, you did it!" She sounded excited as she jumped up and followed them into the kitchen. Over Jane's shoulder, Darce could see Chelsea's expression become worried as Jane opened the kitchen door.

"Jane? What are you doing? Is that my mommy?"

"Don't fret, Chelsea. Your mommy is going to be just fine. You'll really like being with me, and you'll love where you're going. You'll forget, soon enough."

Jane pulled her arm back, preparing to toss Darce through the door, but Chelsea ran up and grabbed the doll.

"No, Jane! You told me you would change her back! It was just s'posed to be a little while!"

Jane rounded on Chelsea and shook her off, sending her tumbling to the floor.

"I'm sorry, but I lied," Jane said. "Oh, who am I kidding? I'm not sorry, at all! I'm finally *free!* But your mommy *is* going to be okay. Nothing can really hurt her."

Then she swung her arm and Darce's world turned upside down, spinning as Darce flipped end over end through the rain. She landed on her back on a soft surface that gave slightly beneath her weight. She stared at the clouded night sky as rain filled her eyes.

The sounds of Chelsea's screams and pleas were faint, coming from inside the house. Darce could only hear them because she was listening so intently. She was sure that no one else would hear them, as the neighbors were either not home or all holed up in their houses, and the rain would muffle the sounds, completely.

After some time, she heard the back door slam, and then the sounds of car doors opening and closing. An engine roared to life.

That's my car!

The car's engine roared and roared as the gas pedal was depressed; then came the sound of the transmission shifting roughly into reverse. A loud *clunk* as the motor stalled out. A couple of more stalls; then the car haltingly backed out of the driveway into the street. The sound of the car slowly receded into the distance.

Darce was alone. Her daughter was gone, and she was helpless to save her.

The moments ticked by and became hours.

At first, Darce railed, raved, and cried inside her prison; but soon enough, she realized that no one would hear her.

Rivulets of rain streamed down her cheeks, and she thought it was appropriate, because they substituted for her own tears, which could no longer fall.

Days passed; then weeks. She watched planes fly overhead, and birds, and butterflies. Occasionally, Darce heard the sound of the phone ringing inside the house. Once in a while, a car would pull into the driveway and someone would knock at the door. Then they would leave.

She often heard the neighbors in their yards, having barbeques or sitting on their porches enjoying the warm weather as their children played outside.

When fall came, the sound of the morning and afternoon school bus provided Darce a kind of time reference. Then the day came that Darce felt a chill on her synthetic skin, just a faint coolness as the temperature continued to drop.

Leaves fell upon her face, blocking her vision. Soon, she felt the sensation of being covered beneath a lightweight blanket that became heavier as time went on. Sounds became more and more muffled and further away; then they disappeared entirely.

Winter had come.

* * *

Darce felt the faint tingle of pins and needles in her pseudo-skin. She was thawing.

She knew that she couldn't let her hopes get too high. A second winter had passed since she had been tossed into the leaf pile. It seemed like an eternity . . . and it could be two more winters before anyone found her. Or four. Or ten.

She couldn't lie there and think of that. It was better to slip into a state of hibernation than to stay awake and alert, with a faint spark of hope in her heart that might never be realized. She sank back down below consciousness. It made the feather-falls of the sands of time drift down a little faster.

She woke again, suddenly, to the sound of a loud vehicle rumbling to a stop. Doors opened and closed, and men shouted back and forth.

"You almost got her, Ron! Okay. Few more steps. That's it, that's it." The sound of heavy footsteps around the side of the house, up the wooden porch steps.

A few moments later she heard more footsteps, coming back outside. More male voices: shouts, conversation.

Still as a stone, she listened.

Another vehicle pulled into the gravel drive. Two car doors opened and then slammed shut. She heard the small, animated voice of a child singing a song; the shuffling of skipping feet and the sound of leaves being kicked up close to Darce's resting place.

Small hands suddenly lifted her upright. Shocked, Darce stared at the freckled face before her. A pair of curious, wide-set, blue-green eyes, tiny rosebud lips, and a snub-nose set perfectly in the center. Ringlets of red hair glowed like an unruly orange halo beneath the bright, mid-spring sunshine.

"Hello!" The little girl smiled. There was a small empty space to the right of her two front bottom teeth. She brushed leaves and dirt from Darce's blue satin dress and smoothed the lace over Darce's bare shins. She passed her hand over Darce's hair and face, wiping away crispy leaf crumbs.

"I'm Rebecca Murphy," the little girl said. "But people call me Becky."

Hello, Becky. My name is Darce. But my little girl used to call me Mommy.

Becky held Darce tightly and ran toward the house.

On this short and bumpy trip, Darce was able to see the world of light and color she had been blind to for so long.

The green grass skimmed by, too tall and weedy with dandelions. The blue sky stretched infinitely above the pines. Small birds, partially hidden in the dense leaves and branches of the hedge, hopped to and fro, twittering. Monarch butterflies fluttered in the air.

"Mom! Mommy! Look what I found!"

Becky thrust the doll forward, holding Darce out for her mother to look at.

Darce felt a shudder of déjà vu as Carol Murphy bent down and scrutinized her face with big, blue-green eyes similar to her daughter's. Her hair was the same shade as Becky's, but fell in loose waves, instead of red ringlets.

"She is very pretty," Carol said. Her forehead wrinkled as she continued her examination. The doll's face looked somehow familiar; dark brown laughing eyes, long black hair. Maybe she'd seen this doll in the toy section of a department store or on a television commercial.

It was wearing some kind of fairy costume, a blue satin dress with blue nylon wings. The dress was covered with small dots of mold.

"But she's really grimy, isn't she?" Carol said. "You know how I feel about bringing strange toys in the house."

"Oh, mommy, please let me keep her! I can give her a bath! She'll be just like new!"

Carol gave Darce a last dubious look, then smiled warmly as she reached over Darce's head to ruffle Becky's red curls. "Maybe we can salvage her. Why don't you take her in right now and give her a bath while I finish unloading these last few boxes? Those clothes are no good, though. You'll have to see if some of your other dolls' clothes might fit her."

Relief flooded through Darce. *Thank God,* she thought.

"Yay! Hooray!" Becky cheered. She twirled around and skipped up the steps and through the back door into Darce's old home.

Before Becky whisked her into the bathroom, Darce caught a quick glimpse at the inside of her house, which greeted her like a long-lost friend. She saw the bulky shapes beneath the dust covers and wondered if they belonged to the same sofa, loveseat, and old overstuffed chair she and Chelsea once cuddled in on rainy nights and during snowy winter weekends.

Becky clicked the bathroom light on and sat Darce on the counter top at the edge of the white porcelain sink. "Now you wait here, Darce," she said, "And I'll go find a washcloth and some soap for your bath." She skipped away, humming to herself.

Darce. She called me Darce! She knows my name! Maybe . . . maybe I can be saved!

But how?

The last time Darce had been so lovingly pampered, it had been as a child, tended to by her mother.

She sat in the sink, immersed in warm, sudsy water while Becky scrubbed her face and body and washed her hair. Afterward, Becky wrapped her in a thick, soft towel and attempted to comb her hair, which was full of snarls.

At least I can't feel the pain, Darce thought as Becky tugged the comb ruthlessly through her thick, black hair.

She was relieved when Mrs. Murphy called to Becky to set her aside for a while and put her belongings away in her new bedroom.

Darce sat and relaxed on the sofa – *her* sofa, with its familiar dark blue cushions.

* * *

Carol had taken vacation from work so that they could accomplish the move. During the next few days, she and Becky busied themselves with unpacking boxes, arranging furniture, and decorating their new home.

Darce enjoyed being with them. They uplifted her spirit with a bittersweet hope. Their compact family of two was so like Darce's own . . . filled with the same daily activities. They watched kids' shows, danced to silly kids' songs or pop tunes on the radio, ate meals of grilled cheese sandwiches and tomato soup and hot dogs and macaroni and cheese, played board games, and had a nightly bedtime routine.

Darce learned that Becky's father had passed away during a tour of duty in Afghanistan. She watched Mrs. Murphy place his photo beside the urn on the fireplace mantel. He had been handsome in his uniform, with dark eyes and a bright white smile.

* * *

Carol had finally gotten most of the household belongings put away; now it was time to take care of the items that weren't currently in use: winter coats and boots, Becky's sled, Christmas and other holiday decorations, and the like. This meant a trip to the attic.

Carol had been to the attic once, when she had viewed the house as a prospective buyer. It had been full of someone else's belongings. From what Carol understood, this clutter had belonged to the previous owner and her daughter, both of whom had disappeared nearly two years before. Most of these items, other than the furniture, had been moved into the attic for storage in the event of the O'Neils' return.

Carol had qualms about buying a house with that kind of history, not the least of which were caused by the similarity between the O'Neils' single-mom-mother-daughter family dynamic and her own. The story gave her chills. It was because of the disturbing history, however, coupled with the fact that she got the house at a tax sale for the low price of two years' worth of back taxes owed, that made it possible for her to afford the house, in the first place. The mortgage on the house had been settled prior to the O'Neils' disappearance.

Every time Carol felt misgivings about her choice in housing, she pushed them away by reassuring herself that she had gotten a steal. It was a lovely house, perfect for her and Becky. It came with all the modern conveniences: a washer and dryer, a dishwasher, central air, nice big back yard, working fireplace. Carol loved her new home.

Still, she couldn't help feeling just a little creeped out as she headed up to the attic. She tried to keep her balance on the narrow wooden steps as she carried the large, awkward box. She was glad that the attic door handle was a lever instead of a knob. This allowed her to push the lever down with her elbow and shoulder the door open without having to put the box down and pick it back up again.

She made it inside the door and, arms trembling with strain, she practically dropped the box to the wooden floorboards, where its impact sent up a small dust cloud. Carol sneezed and waved her arms around to try to dispel the dust. The back of her hand struck something solid that shifted from its resting place and fell to the floor with a *thump.*

She bent to see what object she had displaced. It was a photo album, a little dusty, but not ancient. She squatted to pick it up and rested it on her knees. Curious, she opened it and leafed through the pages.

There were a lot of pictures of a little blonde girl who looked just a little younger than Becky. Christmases, birthday parties . . . first days of school, judging by the neat little dresses she wore as she stood in front of the open door of a school bus in several different photos.

But then Carol's forehead wrinkled when she reached a photo of the little girl with a dark haired woman. Two matching sets of light brown eyes and similar facial features told Carol that this must be the little girl's mother. Her breath caught in her throat.

This must be the missing mother and daughter.

Yes, they were, she decided as she looked further through the album. She remembered the pictures in the local newspaper a few days after they had disappeared.

But there was something about the woman . . .

She stopped again at a professional photo that had been taken of the girl and her mother. They were both dressed nicely for the portrait. The mother wore a light blue satin dress. The picture bothered Carol, but she wasn't sure why. The woman seemed so familiar . . . she shook her head. She just couldn't remember.

She closed the album. She had work to do right now, but later on she would take the time to sort the items in the attic and get them into some sort of order.

She stood and placed the album back on top of the box of items from which it had fallen. In the process, she noticed the corner of another book poking up. She pulled it out. Feeling the textured black cover and seeing the gilt edges of its tissue-thin pages, Carol thought it was a Bible until she opened it and saw unlined pages filled with spidery old handwriting, accompanied by various drawings and diagrams.

Apparently someone's old journal, she thought. *This might be interesting. Might even hold a clue to the mother and daughter's disappearance!*

Or maybe not . . . but Carol was intrigued, and after pushing the box she had carried upstairs out of the way against the wall, she took the book downstairs with her and set it on the side table so that she could peruse the thing in the evening, when the day was settled and she could relax.

She continued sorting and boxing up the items she and Becky wouldn't be using. Remembering her difficulty with the last box she had taken to the attic, she made sure she chose boxes that she could easily carry and that she distributed the weight of the contents more evenly so the boxes wouldn't be too heavy.

"Mommy, can I use your tea kettle? Me and Darce are going to have a tea party, and I can't find mine."

"Sure, sweetheart," Carol replied, "But don't put water in the kettle, okay? *Pretend* tea." She set a box on top of the stack and turned around. She stopped when she saw Becky's doll.

"I thought I told you that old dress was no good," she said. Then she stopped and stared at the doll.

"But I like it . . . it's pretty! And I washed it," Becky added.

"Can I see?" Carol held out her hands. Becky obliged and handed the doll over to her mother.

"You did a very good job washing the dress. It must not have been as damaged as I thought." She smoothed the satin dress, straightened the nylon wings. She passed her hand down the doll's straight, dark hair and wondered at how soft and realistic the shiny tresses felt. She scrutinized its face, touching the cheeks with her fingertips. The skin felt eerily soft and supple, like a child's skin. It felt . . . real.

Wait a minute . . . matching brown eyes . . . facial structure . . .

The doll looked like the mother in the photo album.

That doesn't mean anything. Some people buy dolls that look like them.

A sudden thought struck Carol. She looked at Becky. "What did you say you named her?"

"Darce."

Darce . . . was that the mother's name? "What made you think of that name, Becky?"

"She told me it was her name."

"She *told* you?"

"Yes. I asked 'what's your name', and she thought, '*Darce*'. And I heard her. So I named her that."

"Aaaah. I see." Carol slowly handed the doll back to her daughter, an uneasy feeling settling in the back of her mind. "Does Darce talk often?"

Becky's face lit up. "Oh, yes! She talked to me about Kelsley, her little girl, and the witch, and how she's so unhappy because she's not really a doll, she's trapped in there, and I wish I could help her!"

Carol felt faint. She leaned against the boxes she had just finished stacking against the wall. "Ummm, oh. That's really an interesting story."

"Oh, but I don't think it's just a story, Mommy, I think it's really true! I can't hear my other dolls, we have to pretend talk. But Darce really talks."

"Okay, Rebecca, it's about dinner time. Why don't you and . . . Darce . . . go have your tea party, and you can have some pretend appetizers, and by the time you're all finished, I'll have the main dish on the table, how does that sound?"

"Yay!"

"Tea kettle is on the stove."

"Thank you, Mommy!"

"You are very welcome."

Throughout the rest of the evening, Carol couldn't keep herself from being distracted by the doll. Her eyes were drawn to it. Time and time again, she found herself staring at its face.

At the dinner table, she said to Becky, “No toys at the table. Please take Darce into the living room.”

“But Darce always eats with us, Mommy!”

“No toys at the table has always been the rule. I’ve been letting it slide, but I really would like to stick to it.”

“All right,” Becky said, sounding dejected.

Later, Carol had misgivings as she tucked Becky and Darce into bed. The doll had been creepy to begin with, but now . . . could there be any truth to what Becky was saying?

She had never told Becky about the mother and daughter who had gone missing. She had questioned Becky about places she might have seen that information . . . but the only places she would have access to it would be two-year old newspapers, of which they had none, or the news on television, which Becky ever paid attention to. Or maybe on the Internet . . . which Becky only used for young children’s sites. And Becky hadn’t had any contact with neighbors or with children that might have gone to school with the daughter.

She practically ran up the stairs to the attic and immediately began digging through the same box of items in which she had found the photo album. She knelt on the dusty attic floorboards to make accessing the mess a little easier. Toward the middle of the stack, she found personal papers: medical records, car insurance notices, bills, report cards.

The name on the car insurance notices and bills was Darce O’Neil.

The name on the report cards and medical records was Chelsea O’Neil.

Carol sat back on her heels. The air in the attic was stuffy and oppressive beneath the summer evening sun that beat down on the roof of the house. She wiped the sweat form her forehead with the back of her hand.

So the names Becky told her were correct, almost. She had called Chelsea "Kelsley".

Could her story really be true? Could Darce O'Neil be trapped inside that doll's body? What about the "witch", and Darce's daughter, Chelsea?

She grabbed the photo album and took it downstairs, leaving it with the journal she had brought down earlier. She would look at them both a little later; but right now, she wanted to do an online search to see if she could find any information about the O'Neils' disappearance.

She only found two articles with different dates, both from Singleton's only newspaper. Apparently the mystery wasn't enough to warrant more. They didn't offer much more information than she already had.

Darce O'Neil had failed to show up for work for several days and couldn't be reached by phone. Some of her friends were concerned because they hadn't seen or heard from her since her daughter, Chelsea's, birthday party on August 24, 2009. Chelsea's friends hadn't seen her, either. A missing persons report had been filed on September 9th of that year by Katie Maine, Darce's long-time best friend, prompted by Chelsea's absence the first few days of school.

According to Katie, during none of their conversations about the beginning of the school year had Darce hadn't mentioned that Chelsea would be starting school late.

The two women had even made plans for a picnic at Lake Forshee on the last Saturday in August. Katie and Darce had discussed the picnic after Chelsea's birthday party, when Katie picked up her daughter, Tamara.

But Darce and Katie did not show up for the picnic; nor had Darce returned Katie's phone calls on any day following Chelsea's birthday party.

Darce's car was gone, but all of her and Chelsea's belongings had been left behind, including Darce's cell phone. The birthday party dishes were still dirty, and the television set had been left on. There were no packed bags and no notice to anyone that they were leaving. Police found no clues as to where the two could have gone, and the car was never found.

Seems suspicious to me, Carol thought.

She sat back in her chair and stretched.

Could it be true? A woman trapped inside of a doll, courtesy, no doubt, of the "witch" that Becky had mentioned, who had supposedly kidnapped Darce O'Neil's daughter?

Tomorrow morning, she would ask Becky to tell her a story. One with a lot more details.

But right now, Carol was tired. All this fairytale stuff would have to wait until morning.

* * *

There. That dress.

Carol was once again perusing the photo album. She had wandered into the living room with her coffee and seen it, and the little journal, still lying on the side table where she had left them the day before. She sat and sipped her coffee while she flipped the pages. And stopped when she saw the blue satin dress.

No wings. Same dress.

But that didn't prove anything. Couldn't a custom doll be made with copies of the model's clothing? The doll could have been a gift from a loved one.

She picked up the journal. The pages were so old that she had to handle the book with great care. The corner of one of the pages crumbled between her fingers when she grasped it to turn it. She closed the book. Instead of trying to leaf through it again, this time, she just let it fall open.

The book opened to a page marked by a grungy frayed old purple ribbon she hadn't seen before. She had to squint her eyes to make out some of the handwriting.

"The transition will be made through the Power of Nine: Three words to activate the transition, repeated three times; and three souls: one to articulate the three words, one to be used as sacrifice to release the trapped soul from the Vessel, and one to be retrieved from the Vessel. The sacrificed soul will take the place of the soul released from the Vessel."

* * *

"And she's been inside the doll ever since."

Becky ate a spoonful of her Lucky Charms as she finished telling Darce's story.

"And Darce told you this in your head, with her thoughts."

"Yup!" Becky smiled brightly, a drop of milk dribbling down her chin.

Carol took a sip from her fresh cup of coffee and gazed at Darce, who sat beside Becky's plate on the table.

I'm going to feel like a real idiot if I believe her and it's just a fairy tale.

"Darce says it's *not* a fairy tale, Mommy!"

Startled, Carol almost dropped her cup. "Ummm . . . *what?*"

"Darce says you think her story isn't true, that it's just a fairy tale, but it isn't!"

"How would she know that?"

"She heard you think it!"

"So . . . not only can she think thoughts at you that you can hear, but she can hear your thoughts without you saying them out loud?"

"Yup!" Said Becky.

"Okaaaaay," said Carol. She looked at the doll and thought, *Darce, do you know how to get changed back?*

"No, she doesn't know how," Becky said.

Carol tried again. *Do you have any idea how you got transformed in the first place?*

"She doesn't know that, either. The witch cast a spell on her. But she says that *you* know something."

Carol raised her eyebrows. "Oh?"

"She says you *found* something. A book! A magic book! You found it in the attic! And something about a powder – a powder of mine." Becky wrinkled her nose. "I don't know what she means. I don't have any powder. I had baby powder when I was a baby, but I don't have any anymore 'cause I'm grew, and I'm not a baby now."

Carol set her cup on the table and said quietly, "Do you mean *the power of nine?*"

Becky clapped her hands. "*Yes!*" Her eyes widened and her mouth opened into an "O". "She's right! Darce's right, isn't she? You *did* find something! This means we can help her, right?"

Carol shot Darce a warning glance. "I don't really know, yet. I haven't read enough. I'll have to look at the instructions more thoroughly before I will know for sure."

But she thought, *I'm sorry. This is witchcraft. I'm Catholic. I know nothing about witchcraft. And there has to be a sacrifice. I don't think I can sacrifice anyone.*

Darce sat beside Carol on the sofa that night after Becky had fallen asleep. Carol read the instructions for the "magic spell" out loud.

". . . the Vessel is impenetrable and unbreakable, so whosoever's soul is held captive within cannot die or be destroyed, with one exception. If the Sacrificial Soul is already compromised and ready to pass on, and takes the place of the soul in the Vessel before it has separated from its physical body, this enchantment can be broken

permanently, and the Vessel will be rendered ineffective."

Darce could feel her last seeds of hope drift away into nothingness as she listened. She would never be able to escape her prison without imprisoning another soul. She didn't want to do that; she *wouldn't* do that. And she knew that Carol wouldn't either.

She felt the sensation of Carol's life-sized hand on her small doll-shoulder. "Don't give up just yet, Darce. This may not be easy, but not impossible."

It sounds impossible to me, unless we're willing to kill someone to break the spell, thought Darce. *I don't know which sin would be worse.*

She might as well face the fact that she was going to remain imprisoned in this doll-form forever. Because she couldn't die as long as she was inside it.

She felt her mind drifting away to the shadows where it had spent the past two years.

"We *will* figure it out, Darce," Carol promised, "But look. At least you aren't outside in the dark, alone. You're with me and Becky. And you can still experience things. You can watch television and movies. You can listen to music. We can take you for walks, we can take you places, like shopping and mini-golf. You have a warm, comfortable place to sleep. For now, you're . . . you're paralyzed, but you can communicate. You're still alive, so don't give up yet."

Darce heard what Carol said. She had to admit that Carol was right: with Becky and Carol, she would have kind of a life, even if it was a half-life.

* * *

The half-life continued for several months. They tried to break the spell a few times, in various ways.

Becky brought them an injured butterfly, but by the time they got the ritual space set up with the circle of salt, the candles, water, and soil, the insect had died, and what soul it had, if any, was well on its way to the other side.

After that, they decided to just keep the items set up. Carol had cleared a place in the attic, and would periodically replace the old spell components with fresh ones. They would be ready if they ever received an opportunity.

Their hopes rose when Carol found a wounded bird in the backyard. Unwilling to simply let the creature die if there was a chance it could be saved, however, Carol took care of it as best she could, and they all waited. The bird recovered within a few days, and Carol set it free.

She researched witchcraft and Wicca, trying to educate herself on a subject she had never believed in. It was all pretend, make-believe, not real. Or at least, that's what she had been taught to believe. And now, she questioned her entire belief system.

The more she researched, the more she learned that paganism was not about Satan worship, at all, but more about . . . the worship of nature, and harnessing natural energies to help in the practitioner's endeavors. There were many categories of witches, and though there were some who were self-serving and practiced evil, this wasn't the norm.

Was that so bad? She wasn't really sure what she believed anymore. But she was convinced that this situation could be a reality. If so, then this was what she needed to do.

But still . . . Carol wasn't a witch, and was nervous the first time they tried the spell with the butterfly. She had felt sure something would go wrong. Her hands were shaking and she was sweating.

After that, she practiced the spell over and over until she knew it by heart; the water and earth offerings, the lighting of the candles, the motions, the requests.

* * *

Darce tried not to become frustrated when the start of the school year rolled around and Becky was gone most of the day and Carol was at work. Carol left the television on for Darce and set her in a reclining position on the sofa so that she could either watch TV or doze; but Darce could feel the mounting anguish at not being able to get up to stretch her legs, to walk outside, to even change the channel or put music on, instead.

I am just a living lump, she thought.

She had to force herself to remember that she was no longer in the leaf pile, staring at the sky . . . and then staring into darkness as the leaf pile grew on top of her and the snows obliterated her from sight. That would cheer her a little . . . but only a little, even though she would give her thanks to God, because at least she had been found. Her chances of being saved had increased exponentially.

"Mommy! Mommy! Darce!" The back door slammed and Becky ran into the kitchen, breathless and dirty, her curls tangled from the autumn wind.

Carol sighed impatiently and turned from the stove, where she was stirring the spaghetti sauce for that night's dinner. "Rebecca, how many times have I told you to please not slam the door?"

"But Mommy!" The girl held out her hands. Cupped in her palms was a large maple leaf, upon which lay a small mouse.

Carol bent and examined it closely. Its body was badly damaged and it was trembling. Its frightened little black eyes were wide and shiny. "What happened to it?" she asked.

"There was a cat, and the cat throwed it up in the air and played with it, and when the cat saw me it ran away, and I saw the mouse, and – can we save it?" Tears welled in Becky's eyes.

The mouse's hindquarters and back legs were barely recognizable; the thing was a bloody mess. It was obviously in shock.

"Becky, I don't think we can help this mouse, I'm sorry. But it may be able to help us. Here," she said, taking the leaf and the mouse from Becky. "You grab Darce. Take her straight to the attic and set her down inside the circle. Hurry!"

She quickly turned the burners off and ran behind Becky up the stairs. Under her breath, she chanted, "Please have a soul, please have a soul, please have a soul!" Because she really didn't know if any creatures other than humans had souls.

Once both Darce and the mouse were placed, side by side, within the circle, Carol sent Becky downstairs to watch cartoons.

"But Mommy, I want to see—"

"No, Becky," Carol said firmly. "This could be dangerous. I don't want anyone extra here for this, because things might get mixed up. We should know soon."

"Okay." Becky hung her head, and exited the room.

Carol lit the candles.

She spoke the passages she had memorized. She made offerings of earth and water, made her request, then went silent for a moment as she visualized the outcome, focusing her energy and will.

Darce, inside the circle, focused, as well, putting all of her spirit, thoughts, and heart into her request.

Carol spoke the three words, repeating them three times, as instructed by the book.

"In and out."

"In and out."

"In and out!"

She felt tension build inside of her, and a kind of . . . *energy*, surging simultaneously up from her feet and down through the crown of her head, meeting at her heart.

A sudden clap of thunder made her jump. The sky seized that moment to split open and start dumping torrents of rain down onto the roof. Lightning flashed. The lights went out.

"So mote it be." Carol broke the salt circle with her toe. She felt the release of the tension that had built up within her body as it dispersed into the air. She took a deep breath.

Before her eyes, the doll faded away. In its place lay a woman in a blue satin dress.

Carol stared, shocked. "Oh my God," she whispered.

She had thought that she believed the story – the photos, the names of the vanished mother and daughter, the things Becky had told her as relayed from Darce, the doll. But now, staring at the woman who lay on her back on the attic floorboards – it suddenly struck her that the fairy tale was *real*.

The sound of Becky's voice brought her to awareness. "Mommy! The lights and the TV turned off! I'm sc—Darce? *Darce!* It worked, it *worked!*"

"Becky, wait—"

Becky ran into the circle and flung herself to the floor beside Darce, throwing her arms around her.

The mouse lay beside them on its maple leaf.

The rain abruptly stopped, and the lights came on.

Darce became conscious of the hard floorboards beneath her shoulder blades, and a small, warm body on top of her. It was Becky, and she was sobbing.

"It *worked*, Darce, it *worked!*"

Darce gasped, inhaling the first breath she had taken in over two years. An involuntary shudder went through her body, and she started to cry. Becky and Carol were already shedding tears of joy.

"Becky, honey, please get up off her and give her some space," Carol admonished her daughter gently.

"I'm sorry, Darce," Becky said, sitting back on her heels and wiping her cheeks with her hands.

"Don't be sorry . . ." Darce tried to say, but her throat was dry, her vocal cords contracted from disuse.

"Oh gosh," Carol said. "Becky, please go get Darce a glass of water and a pillow, would you?"

Becky jumped up and ran downstairs, eager to do something to help.

Carol knelt down behind Darce and lifted her head and shoulders onto her lap, to provide an incline to raise Darce's head and help her breathe a little more easily.

Darce tried to help her by sitting up on her own, but found that she couldn't. She rasped, "Oh my God, what's wrong with me?"

"It's okay, Darce," Carol said. "Your motor skills have been dormant for a very long time. "It may take a while for you to be able to move your body normally again."

"I hope so," Darce whispered. It would be tragically ironic to have made it through this ordeal only to find that her body would remain paralyzed.

Becky entered the room with two pillows and a glass of ice water. She helped her mother place the pillows beneath Darce's head and shoulders, and then held the glass to Darce's lips. A little bit of water dribbled down from the corner of her mouth.

But it was so cold, so refreshing against her parched lips and dry mouth. She found that she could lift her head slightly to drink a little more.

Carol started massaging Darce's hands and arms. "Maybe it will help if we try to jump-start your circulation," she said.

When Darce let her head fall back onto the pillows, Becky set the glass down and helped rub Darce's legs and feet.

Soon, Darce started to feel pins and needles throughout her limbs. "I'm finally waking up," she whispered. "Pull me up, please,"

Becky grabbed Darce's hands and pulled while Carol braced herself behind Darce's shoulders and pushed her up. Together, they maneuvered her into a sitting position.

Anticipating what Darce needed next, Becky held the glass up to Darce's lips again. She was able to drink more this time.

"As soon as you're ready, we're going to get you downstairs and into a comfortable bed," Carol said. "You're going to need to rest and recuperate."

Darce let out a small laugh. Her voice was a little stronger when she said, "Rest? That's all I've been doing!"

In a few minutes, the pins and needles tingled throughout her entire body. It was excruciating, and all she could do was lay there, moaning, while tears streamed down her face.

Carol covered Darce with a blanket and wiped her face with a damp washcloth, trying to help comfort her as best she could.

It was about an hour before Darce quieted and the tingling faded away. She was able to assist a little as Becky and Carol half carried, half pulled her down the attic steps to the second floor. The narrow stairwell helped; they were able to use the walls as leverage with which to brace themselves and stay upright.

They managed to lay Darce on the guest bed and propped some pillows behind her back. Becky left the water glass on the bedside table, and Darce found she was able to move her arms enough to pick it up and drink.

Eventually, as reality set in, Darce began sobbing.

Carol, sitting on the bed beside her, asked gently, "Is there anything more that I can do for you right now?"

Darce shook her head, "No."

"I'm going to give you some space and go finish dinner for me and Becky, okay?"

Darce nodded.

"We're right downstairs if you need us."

When she was alone, Darce's body shook as she released two years' worth of pent-up anguish, fear, and grief.

She grieved for Chelsea.

How would she ever find her daughter?

After she had wept out all of the poison, she felt calm. She didn't think that she could sleep after being trapped in that *thing* for the past two years, but she fell into a deep, dreamless sleep nonetheless.

She woke the next morning to a tapping sound. The door opened Becky poked her head inside. "Good morning, Darce! How are you doing?"

"Okay," Darce responded.

"Mommy sent me to bring you some clothes. She said you guys are pretty close in size, so they should fit okay. And she said you should go ahead and have a shower, that it will make you feel like a *million* bucks!"

Darce smiled at the little girl and accepted the small pile of clothing, which smelled pleasantly fresh, like fabric softener.

"I can't believe I have to get used to smelling things again," she said.

Becky smiled. "Mommy's making breakfast and coffee. See you soon!" She skipped out of the room.

Other smells had drifted up the stairs, in through the open door. Darce breathed deeply. Oh God, *bacon!* And . . . *coffee!*

Darce felt her stomach rumble. She was so *hungry*. She tried to swing her legs over the edge of the bed and found that she could move them much more easily than the night before. Walking was still difficult. Her leg muscles hadn't quite gained their muscle memory back, so she used the wall for support as she stumbled her way to the bathroom.

Feeling much refreshed after her shower, she groped her way downstairs, glad for the railing.

In the kitchen, Carol smiled at her and indicated the plate and cup of coffee on the table. Darce practically fell into the chair that had been pulled out for her.

"Thank you so much, both of you," she said. "I am so indebted to you . . . you saved my life."

Carol reached out and squeezed Darce's hand. "No, I want to thank *you.* Because you've helped save mine."

"Wh-what do you mean?"

"Since my husband died, I've just been floating through life like *I* was the ghost. I've barely acknowledged that Becky lost her dad; all I've been thinking about was my own loss. I thought my life was over. But you've made me realize that I still have *so* much left to appreciate, and that the rest of it could disappear like *that.*" She snapped her fingers. "Besides," she continued, "I'm sure you would have done the same for me. When faced with a difficult situation, what is one to do except rise to the occasion? I feel so horrible for you. I can't imagine being trapped in that thing for two years. I can't believe you're still sane!"

"I'm not so sure that I *am* sane," Darce replied. And then, feeling shamed, she said, "Jane spent nearly a hundred and fifty years inside it, and I never offered her a kind or generous thought."

"But she was evil! She did horrible things to you and your daughter! I can't imagine anything like that happening to my child. And everything happened so *fast*."

Darce stared into her coffee.

"I'm so sorry, Darce," Carol said. "I know it's painful, but we need to talk about it. For your sake . . . and your daughter's."

Darce had thought she'd run out of tears the night before, but she felt her eyes stinging. She blinked the unshed tears away. The time for crying was over.

"I know. I just don't know what to *do*. I might have some money, if the bank hasn't closed my account. But . . . no job. No idea where to begin to look for Chelsea. No place to live . . ." she shook her head.

"Darce . . . Becky and I would really like it if you stayed here, with us. This would still be your home if this nightmare hadn't happened to you. You're going to need to start over. We want to help you."

Becky, who had been sitting quietly, chimed in. "Yeah, Darce! And then when we find Kelsley – I mean, *Chel*sea, she can live here, too, and we can be like sisters and play together! Say you'll stay, Darce, say you'll stay!"

"If you're sure—"

"We've never been so sure of anything."

Darce let out a breath of relief. "Thank you so, so much!"

"And," Carol said, with a small smile, "When we find Chelsea, guess who else we'll find? Your wicked witch."

Darce looked at her for a moment. "Jane," she said.

Carol held out her cup. "Cheers!"

They clinked their cups together and drank.

"Um . . . Mommy?" Chelsea held up a shoebox that she'd been holding on her lap.

"Oh, right!" Carol set her cup down. "We are going to give our mouse savior a proper burial."

"Her name is Josie." Becky lifted the lid from the box. The three of them looked inside at the small gray rodent lying still on the maple leaf.

Darce reached in and caressed the mouse's head with her finger. "This is what saved me? Everything happened so fast, I never even saw him. He's so tiny."

"Josie's a girl!" Becky interjected.

Carol nodded. "It's amazing how the very least of us can hold so much power. I questioned whether it even had a soul."

"Mommy! *Everything* has a soul!" Becky scolded.

"Honey, some religions hold the belief that only humans have souls."

"Really?'

"Well, now we know differently."

Darce cleared her throat. "I think that we should give her a sendoff fit for a queen. She's a little heroine."

"Yeah!" Becky jumped up from her chair. "I want to give her a blanket so she stays warm. And cheese, so she has something to eat. And water!"

Her mother laughed. "Okay, okay! Why don't you gather your items while Carol and I finish breakfast. Then we'll go out and bury him. I mean, *her*."

In the back yard, Carol suggested they bury Josie beneath the tree where Becky had found Darce. Darce was adamant that they bury the mouse elsewhere. "I wouldn't wish that leaf pile on any creature, living or dead. What about near the foot of the rose bush?"

Becky clapped her hands. "That's perfect! Josie will like the pretty roses and their smell and the sunshine!"

"You got it!" Carol agreed.

She found an old spade of Darce's in the basement and dug a hole just out of reach of the roots of the rose bush. Each of them said a few words, then shoveled a spade full of soil atop the lid of the shoe box.

When Darce's turn came, she said, "Farewell, little friend. The life you lost was not in vain. You are a tiny creature who performed a giant service. I owe you my life. Thank you." Tears stung her eyes as she filled in the small hole with the remaining soil.

Carol grasped Darce's hand in her own. "So mote it be," she said.

GREEN THUMB

"Uh-uh. No way!" Geraldine slashed the air with her arm. "Put those pamphlets away. I am *not* leaving this house."

Julie sighed and swept the pamphlets off the table and into her purse. "Mother, we're just trying to look out for you –"

"Really?" The older woman asked derisively. "Where were you when I had breast cancer?"

"It's because of that –"

"Where *were* you?" Geraldine interrupted. "You knew about it. You knew about the mastectomy. Did I even get a phone call? A visit in the hospital? *A get well card?* "

"Mother, I'm sorry."

"It's too late for that. That was four years ago. *Four years!* Long enough for my hair to grow back. You're lucky I let you back into this house. You abandoned me when I needed someone, anyone, to stand by me. And now that I'm fully recovered, you want me to go to an *old folks' home?*"

Julie sighed and rolled her eyes. "They are assisted living facilities. You would still be independent, but there would be people there to help you."

"What are you, fifteen? Don't roll your eyes at me," her mother snapped. "*Facilities.* You might as well lock me up in an institution! I don't need a babysitter."

Geraldine wasn't about to tell Julie that she was on medication for both her heart *and* high blood pressure.

Standing at the sink, she looked out the window as she washed their lunch dishes. She watched as Julie's husband, Scott, rode the lawn mower around her yard beneath the summer sun. He was wearing headphones. "I know that idiot is behind this. It was *his* fault you didn't come. He thinks I'm stupid. I know he wants this house and my land. And *you* aren't very smart, letting him convince you to railroad me into an old folks' home." She paused. "What is he doing out there, anyway?"

Julie turned and clicked the buttons on each side of the high chair tray, sliding it out so that she could pluck six month-old Susie from the seat and deposit the baby onto her lap. "He's being nice. He thought he would do you a favor."

"*Oh!*" The teacup Geraldine was holding suddenly fell from her hand and shattered on the kitchen floor.

"It's only a teacup, Mother. Mother?" Julie grabbed Susie and followed Geraldine to the screen door, which slammed in her mother's wake.

Julie watched Geraldine pelt across the green lawn, her red plaid shirt and thick, steel-colored braid flying out behind her. She reached the riding lawn mower, waved her arms and screamed, "What are you doing? Stop! *Stop!*"

Scott saw her, smiled, shut the mower off, and lifted up the headphones. "Hi, Geraldine. It's a nice day for mowing the lawn. How does she look?" He said proudly. Then, he noticed her red face and angry expression. "Is everything okay?"

Her palm connected with his face, and a resounding *slap!* echoed across the yard.

"*Mother!*" The screen door slammed again as Julie came out and trotted to where her mother stood and her husband sat on the mower, shocked, one hand to his cheek.

"Ow! What the hell was that for?"

"You idiot! You just mowed down one of my new annual beds!"

"Mother!" Julie tried to intervene. "That doesn't mean you just smack him like that!"

Geraldine rounded on her, her pointed, skeletal face livid. "*YOU!* You brought him here! He just ruined weeks of hard work. My gardens are all that I have. He's trying to take everything from me!"

Scott turned to Julie. "Damn, is this how she raised you?"

"*Get out!*"

Julie stared, her blue eyes round. "Mother, you can't mean –"

"I mean it. All of you. Get out! If you ever come back here, don't bring *him!*"

Susie started crying. Scott dismounted from the mower, his face red. "Geraldine, I'm really sorry. I was just trying to help you. But I'd like to point out that you are a miserable, ungrateful old bitch!"

"Just *go*. Leave me be!"

"Gladly!" Scott threw the lawnmower key down on the seat. "Come on Julie, you heard her. Let's get out of here!"

Geraldine stalked into the house. She sat down hard on the sofa and breathed deeply, trying to get her racing heartbeat under control. She heard Julie go into the kitchen to grab Susie's diaper bag and bottle. Then the car doors slammed, and the engine roared to life. The sound receded into the distance.

Emotionally drained, she lay down and pulled the afghan over her. When she felt better, she would go outside and check the scope of the damage and see what, if anything, she could do to salvage her flowerbed.

* * *

Geraldine started awake. The glowing letters on her digital clock read 1:16 a.m. She listened intently, trying to determine what had disturbed her sleep. The house was quiet.

Too quiet.

She threw her covers aside and slipped out of bed and into her slippers. She moved through the living room across the hardwood floor, her vision acclimating quickly to the moonlit room. She paused to listen again, but all she heard was the faint hum of the refrigerator.

She retrieved the key from the coffee cupboard and unlocked the gun cabinet in the living room. Holding her rifle, she stepped out the back door. The motion-activated floodlight switched on, bathing her backyard and gardens in too-bright artificial light. With an oath, she ran down the back step to her vegetable gardens.

All of her carrots, which had just begun sprouting, had been pulled and cut to pieces; likewise, her tiny cucumbers and lettuce heads. Her tomatoes, still small, yellow, and hard, had all been picked and stomped into a yellow mess in the green grass.

Her jaw tightened as she scanned the yard. She saw no one.

Crack! She fired a warning shot into the air and screamed, “You’ll pay for this!”

Her heart felt like it was going to pound right through her chest. She needed to calm down. She took some deep breaths, turned and walked back into the house, locking the door behind her.

She sat up for a while in the dark living room, waiting and listening. Eventually, she fell asleep beneath her sofa afghan.

Now she had two wasted garden beds to fix.

The following night, it was her Asiatic Lilies. They had been yanked out by the roots and left scattered across the lawn. To top it off, a rock had been thrown through the mud room window. Pieces of shattered glass had fallen inside Geraldine's boots and sneakers.

She called the police. The county sheriff came out, viewed the damage, took her statement and filed a report. He said he would have a car come out and cruise by periodically.

* * *

Geraldine pulled the containers out of the shipping box. The small flower pots wore clear plastic bubble lids to protect the plants that protruded from the soil. Or maybe the lids were to protect people from the plants. The containers reminded her of the novelty Venus Fly Traps she'd seen before at pharmacies and dollar stores.

She examined one of the labels. "Amazonian Dart," she read. "Grows rapidly, producing brilliant fire-red blossoms. Thrives in containers and in ground. Full sun. Water generously at least three times per week. Blah, blah, blah." She read down further. "Use caution when tending to full-grown plant. Cover plant entirely with a cloth when in close proximity. Full-grown plant uses heat sensors to detect predators, then shoots small darts to immobilize them. Darts may travel a distance up to approximately 2'. Poison is extremely toxic and in some cases may be fatal, particularly to smaller animals. Keep away from children and pets."

She smiled. "These should work just fine. Or at least, they'd better, at $250 each."

She had lost another perennial bed by the time she put the darts in the ground. She planted them strategically and inconspicuously.

She wouldn't let Scott scare her out of her home.

* * *

Geraldine yawned and stretched. Sunlight streamed around her window shade. She looked at her clock and was surprised to see that it was 6:11 in the morning. She had gotten her first full night's sleep in weeks.

She made her way to the kitchen and coffee. Cup in hand, she stepped out the back door to view her gardens.

She paused when saw something lying on the grass in front of one of the dart plants. Curious, she grabbed a bath towel and a pair of gardening gloves. She approached the plant, tossed the towel over it and knelt to examine the robin. It had what looked like a needle poking out of its red breast. She picked the robin up with one gloved hand and held it at eye level for a closer look.

It wasn't exactly a needle; it was a tiny clear quill-like cylinder, about two inches long. The end that protruded from the robin's breast was dark brown. She pulled at it with her fingertips, extracting it easily. The tip that came out, red with blood, was pointed and looked extremely sharp.

"Tch," she said. "So this is one of its poison darts. What a shame, poor little thing. Still," she sighed, "I guess in a situation like this, there's bound to be a little collateral damage."

She took the robin and the dart to the bare bed of soil where Scott had mowed down her annuals. She cleared a hole with her hands about a foot deep, deposited the robin and the dart at the bottom, and filled in the hole. "Rest in peace. I'm sorry," she said.

She went back to where the covered plant grew at the Southwest corner of her house. She had read the package instructions further before she had planted the Amazonian dart flowers; she knew to stand out of the way of the plant's trajectory, which was limited to targets directly in front of it.

She reached out and gingerly pulled the towel back just enough so that she could lean over and view the plant from above.

She had already seen the bouquet of red blossoms. The shape of each bloom resembled that of a daffodil, except there were several blooms on each stem, as opposed to one. She hadn't previously seen the darts, themselves, and was curious as to how they grew. The anatomical structure of the flowers had not been included in the package information.

It looked as though, where a daffodil had an anther atop a filament, these flowers had the needle-like cylinders, or "darts", and, similar to the daffodil, there was a tiny pod atop the dart that seemed a parallel of the anther, which held the pollen in the daffodil. There was one dart per each bloom.

The plant's toxin must be stored in the pod at the tip of the dart. And the pod apparently stayed behind in the body of the target predator when the dart was pulled away.

But where was the pollen stored? How were the flowers pollinated?

She shrugged. She supposed it didn't matter.

She grasped the corner of the towel and backed up a couple of large steps, holding the towel in front of her, just in case she stepped within range of the plant's sensors.

At least she knew the plants worked. Purchasing items from an 800-number on a television commercial, in her opinion, was a foolish thing to do. But after what Julie's husband (Geraldine would never call him son-in-law) had done to her gardens, she had to see for herself if these flowers were for real. And they were perfect. Sitting innocently in her garden, looking lush and beautiful, they would deliver a surprising and painful message.

Satisfied, she went into the house to clean up for dinner and relax a little in front of the television.

"Still a pity about the robin, though," she said as she closed the back door behind her.

Except that it didn't stop with the robin.

Two days later, Geraldine found a dead rabbit lying on the ground a couple of feet in front of the second dart flower. This time, when she examined the rabbit, she found three darts lodged in the body: two in the chest, one in the left cheek.

Her eyebrow furrowed as she removed the darts. "More darts for larger animals?" she murmured. She looked at the darts in her palm, then at the limp rabbit.

She didn't particularly like rabbits, and there were plenty that liked to come and steal from her vegetable gardens. Garden fencing usually took care of the problem, though, and she did like to look out her kitchen window and see the wildlife that frequented her yard.

Three darts, though.

She would have skinned and cooked the rabbit, but she didn't know if the toxin would affect her, so instead, she buried the rabbit beside the robin. She had already decided to leave the ravaged plot alone for the remainder of the season. She would plant bulbs there in the fall.

She heard the faint sound of her phone ringing, and hurried inside. "Hello?"

"Hello, Mother."

"Julie," Geraldine acknowledged.

"I was just checking up to see how you're doing."

"I'm fine."

"Oh, because we had heard something about break-ins or vandalism out around where you live, and we were kind of worried."

"Really?" Geraldine tried to sound surprised. "Well, I'm perfectly fine, and I haven't heard a thing."

"Okay. I just want you to know that we're here if you ever need us."

"Wonderful, Julie, thank you."

They engaged in brief small talk . . . how are you doing, etc.; then Geraldine bid her daughter goodbye and hung up.

As if she was ever going to allow Julie's husband back on her property.

Her mouth set in a thin, grim line, Geraldine dialed her attorney's number. It was about time she changed her will. If she had any say in it, Scott would never have a piece of this house or her property.

Her attorney wasn't available; he was with a client, so she just left a message.

* * *

Geraldine sat up in bed. She had definitely heard a noise through the light rain that tapped on the roof.

She grabbed her robe, and instead of her slippers, she pulled on her rubber gardening boots in the mud room. She stepped out the back door.

The flood lights came on, illuminating the back lawn, sparkling wet with rain. She heard a moan, a familiar female voice. She scanned the yard.

There. The floodlights glowed against a halo of blonde hair. Someone was lying on the ground at the corner of the house.

Geraldine gasped. "Julie?" She ran down the steps and along the back of the house. "Oh my God, he sent you to do this!"

She reached the inert form.

Julie was dressed in black jeans, boots, and a dark brown rain coat. She lay on the ground, moaning. In her fist, she clutched a handful of stems. Amazonian Dart stems. Bright red blossoms lay scattered on the ground.

"*Julie!*" Geraldine dropped to the ground and gathered her daughter into her arms, oblivious to the lethal plant just beside her.

"M-m-m-mother, it wasn't Scott . . . h-h-hurts . . ."

"Where did it hit you?" Geraldine leaned back to look at Julie. The front of her rain coat was littered with protruding darts. "Oh, no . . . oh no . . ." She pulled one out with her bare fingers. The tip was red with blood. She pulled another and another. They had all pierced Julie's rain coat and the light sweater she had worn beneath. There were at least ten. The plant had released all of its darts.

Geraldine's eyes stung with tears. She shook her daughter, whose head lolled limply. "Julie! Julie! Do you have your cell phone? Where is your cell phone?"

"P-p-po . . . p-p-pock . . ."

Geraldine rifled through Julie's coat pocket and pulled the phone out. She dialed 9 1 1 with wet fingers.

"Nine-one-one, what's your emergency?"

"Julie, Julie's going to die, she's poisoned, help us!"

"Okay, try to be calm ma'am. Who is Julie?"

"Julie's my daughter." Geraldine's breath came raggedly. Her chest had tightened, and pain was spreading across her back and down her right arm.

"Okay, what is your name?"

"Geraldine." More pain.

"And what is your address?"

Geraldine collapsed on top of Julie, the cell phone falling from her hand.

"Hello? Geraldine? Geraldine?"

* * *

Scott stood in Geraldine's backyard and surveyed the gardens that had been so precious to her. He held Susie in one arm and an umbrella in the opposite hand. The rain fell down in fat, sloppy drops. He sighed. The listing papers had been signed; the "For Sale" sign was firmly planted next to the front walk.

He had never cared about Geraldine's property, but it had driven Julie crazy that her mother "hoarded" it – or so, Julie had thought. She felt she deserved the house and the 15 acres that came with it. Scott was just as satisfied with their apartment. It was a nice apartment, spacious, clean, well-maintained, close to stores and the community playground. He never thought they needed more. And if they had, he would have wanted them to buy a new place, one that they could make their own. But Julie kept trying to get her mother put away so that they could move in here.

Now, Scott wanted no part of it. Because of his wife's greed, his mother-in-law's stubbornness and the pair's vindictiveness, he had lost his wife. Susie had lost both her mother and her grandmother.

He had already purchased a new home for himself and Susie with the funds he had inherited from the mess. He was taking his little girl home to upstate New York, where he had grown up and still had family.

As he turned to leave, he noticed the large patch of soil where he had mowed down Geraldine's flowerbed. Several new green shoots protruded from the otherwise bare patch of dirt.

"I don't see why she made a big deal," he said to his daughter. "Looks like those flowers I cut down are growing back, anyway." At the same time, looking out over the colorful blooms and ornamental grasses, he kind of understood Geraldine's reaction to what he had done – even though it had been an honest mistake.

He shook his head. It didn't matter to him, now. "Well, this is it, Susie-Q. Let's go." He bounced the baby in the crook of his arm as he walked away.

BEREAVEMENT SERVICES, LLP

Juniper wiped through the foamy fog of lemon-scented furniture polish, clearing it from the sideboard's surface until the walnut finish glowed. There; the dusting was done.

She had gotten the daily chores down to a science, and what had once taken the better part of each day now took only a couple of hours, leaving the rest of the day free. Simon didn't know that, though, and Juniper wasn't about to volunteer the information. He thought she spent all of her time slaving away.

That's the way it had been during the first few months of their marriage. He had loaded her down with so many tasks that it was nearly impossible to complete them all by 5:30 p.m., when he came home from work. She was often sweaty and disheveled, dinner either still cooking or burned, the kitchen a mess, when he walked through the door.

Eventually, Juniper managed to coordinate everything and became efficient at her work. She completed the chores with time to spare, and used that extra time for herself. She read books, watched television, or relaxed on the rear patio with a drink, observing the comings and goings of the wildlife in the woods and fields that surrounded the house. Simon came home every evening to a hot, perfectly prepared dinner awaiting him on the polished and elegantly set dining room table.

After a few days of being greeted coolly at the door, Simon questioned how his pretty young wife was spending her days. At the time, she was unaware that he *wanted* her to be flustered, frazzled, and exhausted, running around the house in a panic, trying to get things done by the time he arrived.

He had not been pleased at Juniper's explanation of efficiency. The reprimand, as usual, was physically harsh, and he doubled her list of chores, practically pushing her out of bed the next morning to start work despite her freshly bruised ribs.

He shook his finger at her. "Don't ever let me catch you sitting around reading worthless smutty romance novels or watching television," he said. "I didn't marry you to use up my electricity watching Jerry Springer and those other idiotic reality shows all day long."

His newly wedded wife didn't bother to argue that she watched the History and Discovery channels, not reality television. Nor did she correct him and tell him that she read books from his own library; it really would have hit the fan, then. She had learned enough of his obsessive-compulsive habits to make sure every book looked untouched when she returned it to its shelf each day.

She had also learned enough to remain silent about why she thought he had married her, to begin with: she had thought he'd loved her. He had been good to her when they met. A gentleman. Well-mannered. Generous. Attentive. Affectionate.

But as soon as they had crossed the threshold of his home, the crash course in Simon Kurst's marriage practices had begun. She was, for all intents and purposes, his servant. His possession. To use as he saw fit.

The honeymoon, as they say, was over.

Juniper learned many things early on in her marriage, such as how not to speak unless spoken to; how not to argue; how to correctly clean the house, wash the clothes and dishes, dust the furniture. Everything had to be done exactly to Simon's specifications, and the smallest details were subject to Simon's meticulous daily inspection – down to the measuring and marking of the liquid laundry detergent bottle.

The one thing she didn't worry about were the already opened wine bottles. The glass was too dark for Simon to see the levels of the liquid inside, so he didn't mark them. He marked the vodka, the scotch, and the rum bottles. Juniper didn't like any of those, so she never had to worry about replacing the contents of any of them.

One of her lessons was that even though Simon expected perfection of Juniper, he was suspicious when he received it. What she learned from this were which trace items to leave undone: enough to allay his suspicions, but not enough to earn extreme punishment.

Six years later, however, nothing had changed – except for Juniper. Finding herself repeatedly on the receiving end of Simon's unpredictable and inescapable rage, she had become increasingly rebellious, though she didn't show it. Where once she had been soft and loving, she had become hard and indifferent. She was just waiting for her moment: to do what, she wasn't sure.

Now, as she opened the sideboard drawer and prepared to polish the silver, she heard the familiar drone of the mail truck, which drove by every day at quarter past eleven. It never stopped there. All of the mail went to Simon's office or to his post office box.

When the sound of the truck's motor slowed, failing to fade into the distance, Juniper left the silver and peered out the bay window. She watched as the small, square truck drove carefully down the driveway and stopped. Cutting the engine, the mail carrier jumped out.

She reached the door just as the knock came.

The mail carrier held a small envelope. "Are you Mrs. Juniper Henry Kurst?" he asked her. She nodded, and he indicated where she should sign on the green and white receipt. He tore it off at the perforations, handed her the envelope, and touched his cap. "Have a good afternoon, ma'am."

After the truck had reversed up the driveway and trundled away, Juniper turned the envelope over. It was an off-white greeting card envelope, roughly textured, addressed to her and lacking a return address. She hesitated only a second before she tucked it into her back pocket and grabbed the hose to wash the mail truck's dusty tire tracks from the driveway. The heat of the summer sun would dry the asphalt long before Simon came home from work.

Inside, Juniper sat on the sofa and slid her finger along the edge of the flap, separating it from the envelope. She pulled out a card that matched the envelope, along with a self-addressed, stamped return envelope. On the card were penned a few short lines, together with a return address. The card was signed "Uncle Drew".

Her heart fluttered with joy and her spirit lifted. Uncle Drew was not her real uncle, but her father's best friend, so he may as well have been family. They had grown fond of each other when she was growing up.

She sat for a moment, contemplating the postmark and thinking about what this really meant.

During the first few months of her marriage, the newly wedded Juniper had often thought of Andrew, wishing there were some way she could contact him. She needed help, but didn't know how to get it. Her parents were both deceased, and Simon's isolation tactics had succeeded in driving away the two or three good friends she'd once had. Now she was alone, with no one at her back. She wasn't permitted to drive any of Simon's three vehicles or to use the telephone, unless it was a call she was making for him or if he was close by, listening in. She was flat-out banned from using the internet.

She never attempted to do any of those things, for fear that her husband would find out. He often warned her that if she tried to leave him, he would kill her.

Juniper believed him.

She had never thought of the solution that stared her in the face for six years, so obvious that she could have kicked herself. The old mailbox at the top of the driveway, sitting abandoned and unnoticed. Finding stamps might have been a problem . . . but still, the United States Postal Service held the key.

Juni, you're an idiot, she thought, echoing Simon's favorite put-down.

She glanced at the clock. It was quarter to twelve! She needed to send a reply. She had too much left to do right now, however – including finding a hiding place for her post card.

She went upstairs into their bedroom and scanned for an inconspicuous spot. Finally, she decided on the carpet that covered the hardwood beneath their bed.

With some effort, she lifted the left corner of the bed. She slid the envelope between the hardwood and the carpet, at the corner, pushing it far in, beyond where the bed frame's foot would rest. She lowered the foot gently down and stepped back to inspect the carpet.

It looked completely undisturbed.

* * *

Simon blinked groggily. His head throbbed. He turned over, pulling the blanket to cover him, and became aware of his sore arms – a steady ache that spread down through his hands. He raised his right hand to look. His knuckles were swollen and smeared with dried blood.

His slight groan brought the pounding in his head to a furious crescendo. With his knee, he nudged his wife, who lay next to him on top of the covers, still wearing yesterday's clothes.

"Juni, go get me an ice pack and some pain killers. I'm wicked hungover." When she didn't stir, he nudged her harder. "Juni, come *on*!"

She didn't move.

"Dammit," he said, and sat up. Vertigo rushed through his head and nausea roiled in his stomach. He sat very still for a moment, willing both sensations to go away. When he felt a little more stable, he reached over and shook Juniper, wincing at the pain in his knuckles. "Wake up, lazy ass, I need some pain killers!"

When there was still no reaction, Simon cursed again and threw off his blankets. He swung his legs over the edge of the bed and felt for his slippers with his feet. Not finding them, he gingerly tilted his head and looked down. Juniper had forgotten to set his slippers next to the bed.

Worthless! He thought.

He stumbled around, searching. When he found the slippers, he shoved his feet into them and made his wobbly way to the bathroom.

The pain in Simon's head made it difficult for him to focus as he rifled through the medicine cabinet. He finally found some acetaminophen and swallowed four of the tablets. Drinking from the cup he kept on the bathroom sink, he chased them down with lukewarm tap water. A wave of nausea washed over him and he clung to the edge of the sink, sweating.

Man, what a hangover! He needed something in his empty stomach.

"Juniper!" He called. "Get up and make me some breakfast!" He listened for a response, for the sounds of Juniper stirring. He heard nothing. Sighing, he looked at himself in the mirror above the sink. Squinting, bloodshot brown eyes looked back at him, the lines in the skin around them seeming somehow deeper than they had the day before.

He used the toilet and gave his hands a cursory rinse. The broken, torn skin on his knuckles smarted beneath the running water.

He stumbled back into the bedroom, to the side of the bed where his wife still lay sleeping.

"You're really letting me down, here, Juni. You know what happens when you let me down." Ignoring his aches and pains, he grabbed her shoulder and shook her forcefully.

He suddenly drew his hand back. Something didn't feel right. Her shoulder, her arm . . . felt . . . *rigid.* And not even lukewarm. "Oh, shit," he said.

Simon bent to examine her more closely. Her honey colored hair looked rusty, stiff with dried blood. He pushed it away from her face. The black and blue bruise around her eye stood out against her pale skin, as did the dried blood that had dripped down her cheek and down the front of her white shirt. He put his hand under her nostrils, but failed to detect a warm breath. He lowered his ear to her nose and mouth and listened, again trying to detect a puff of breath, but none came. He put his palm flat against the fabric at the middle of her chest, but felt no heartbeat. Neither did he feel a pulse beneath his fingers against her chill, stiff wrist.

Nothing.

He threw his hands in the air. His thin lips flattened across his narrow, tan face. His brow furrowed, deepening the already permanent ruts across his forehead. *Stupid woman should have known better than to piss me off!* It was her own fault.

Now, Juniper had put him into a delicate position. He had to figure out what he was going to do with her. And he had to figure out who was going to take care of his house. *Who's going to cook, wash my clothes? At least she could do that . . . and keep house. Now I have to waste money and pay someone. Until I'm remarried.*

And what about the criminal part of it? Simon was smart enough to know that law enforcement wouldn't be reasonable enough to realize that he had simply punished Juniper for her disobedience and that her death was the result of her own actions. *It was her own fault.* Hell, it was more or less suicide.

At least she didn't have any friends and family that he needed to worry about. Still, if Juniper just disappeared completely, there would be questions.

Hands on his bony hips, Simon stared down at his wife's lifeless form.

He could get rid of her body and say that she had disappeared, that she had left him. Why not? *No body, no evidence, no crime, right? Isn't that how it goes?*

That's what he would do. Get rid of Juniper's body.

But before he took care of the details, he would have a good breakfast, even if he had to make it himself. He would need his strength for the morning's activities. Then was going to clean himself up. A nice hot shower would make him feel like a new man.

The painkillers had kicked in, and Simon felt somewhat normal again. Cheered that he had formed a plan of action, he whistled as he shrugged into his robe and tied it as he headed downstairs.

He stumbled down the last three steps when he saw the man sitting in his favorite easy chair in the living room.

Clean-shaven and dressed in a shiny suit that easily cost a month's worth of Simon's sizeable salary, the man was examining his impeccably manicured fingernails. A roaring fire burned in the fireplace beside him, signifying that he had been there for quite a while. Despite the fire, there was a distinct lack of the scent of burning wood. Instead, the whole room smelled like sulfur, as though a match had just been blown out.

When he saw Simon, the man smiled. "Ah, good," he said, and unfolded the length of his tall body from the recliner. He approached Simon, holding out his hand for Simon to shake. A blue vapor surrounded him, rising in faint trails from his extended fingertips. "You must be Simon Kurst, then. Very pleased to meet you."

Simon stepped slowly forward. He ignored the intruder's outstretched hand. "Who are you and what are you doing in my house? How did you get in?"

"Oh, I apologize for my lack of manners. My name is Andrew Smite, of Dieter, Worthem, and Smite, Bereavement Services, LLP." His smile disappeared and he knitted his dark eyebrows in concern. "You *are* bereaved, aren't you, Mr. Kurst? I have the understanding that you recently lost your beloved young wife."

"I don't know how you got in my house, but you are trespassing. If you leave immediately, I won't call the authorities," Simon offered.

"Come now, Mr. Kurst, let us not be hasty." Smite folded himself into Simon's easy chair and settled back comfortably. "I *did* knock, after all, and no one answered. The door was left ajar, so I simply let myself in. I can see that you find my presence unnerving. Be that as it may, I don't think that now is the most prudent time to call the police. Do you?" He looked at Simon with sharp, gray eyes. "I don't understand why you have no security . . . a man of your means, even if you do reside miles from civilization."

Simon stared as the blue vapor rose from the surface of the man's elegant clothing. "I also took the liberty of stoking your fire," said Smite smoothly, nodding at the fireplace. "It was quite chilly in here, and I wasn't sure how long I would be required to wait for you to make an appearance."

Simon suddenly noticed the rivulets of sweat that rolled down his back. "Now is not exactly a very good time, Mr. Smite. I have things to –"

"On the contrary, Mr. Kurst," Smite interrupted. "I think that now is the very best time. After all, young Mrs. Kurst *has* just recently departed, hasn't she? We've found that the earlier we can intervene to offer our services, the more satisfied our clients are, and the outcome is so much better for everyone, all around." His bright white smile flashed against his tan face.

Prickles of sweat broke out on Simon's forehead. *How* did Smite know? Why the hell was he here?

Smite picked up a manila folder from the coffee table beside him. "I think that you might find the contents of this file rather interesting. It would be unfair of me to leave you without giving you the opportunity to peruse them." He stood and offered Simon the folder.

Simon readied himself to protest, but something in Smite's demeanor stopped him. He eyed the folder nervously. He reached out and grasped its corner between his thumb and forefinger, as though the paper was something disgusting that he didn't really want to touch.

"You may want to sit down before you look at what's inside," Smite advised.

Shooting the intruder a dirty look, Simon moved to the sofa and sat. He opened the folder and saw one sheet of paper – and one photograph. Viewing the image, Simon cursed.

In the photo, Juniper lay on the living room carpet in the fetal position, her arms raised to protect her face. Simon stood over her, his foot just making contact with her stomach.

Beads of sweat now rolled down from his hairline as he looked up and studied Smite intently for a moment: the slicked-back gray hair, the expensive suit, the aura of money that surrounded the man. He could sense something dark and slithery beneath the surface. "Where did you get this?" Simon demanded.

"I am not at liberty to discuss where the photo came from; however, it exists, as do many others." The man smiled widely, the carnivorous smile of a shark. "In addition, Mr. Kurst, my partners are aware that I am here and that I'm meeting with you. If you should entertain any bright ideas, it will be all over for you by nightfall."

"What do you want from me? Money?"

"Come, now, Mr. Kurst. Do I look like I need money? Even more, do I look like the type of man who would stoop to underhanded measures to get it?"

I'm not so sure about that, Simon thought. "Why are you here, then? You must want *something* from me. Otherwise, you would have taken your photo – oh, excuse me – *photo-zuh* – to the police."

Smite sighed heavily. "You misunderstand me, Mr. Kurst. My company does not *take* from the grieving; we do everything we can to *give*. I am here to offer you an opportunity to redeem yourself. You *do* feel remorse for what you've done, don't you?

Remorse. *Did* he feel remorse? He supposed he did. After all, Juniper had always taken care of him. She made good food, kept the house and the laundry clean, and was available for sex. If he hadn't killed her, Simon wouldn't now be worrying about who was now going to fill her role. Or about going to prison.

"Oh, for Devil's sake, man!" Simon jumped at Smite's thundering voice. "That isn't usually a question people have to *think* about! What is wrong with you?" The tall man's lips turned down at the corners in an ominous frown. His gray eyes bored into Simon's.

His nervousness giving way to full-fledged fear, Simon replied, "Well, yeah, I feel remorse. It should go without saying, shouldn't it?"

"Unless you're a lying psychopath," Smite retorted. "Just read the paper."

Simon unfolded the sheet of paper and skimmed it. "I, Simon Kurst, do agree to take Juniper Kurst back into my home as living . . ." he looked at Smite. "What is this? It looks like a contract. And how can I take her back?"

Smite rolled his eyes in exasperation. "My business offers some very special services. We provide grief counseling, re-entry programs for those who need help to get back on their feet after the death of a spouse, and so on. This is one of our more 'special' services, which we offer to only a select few. People like you who have lost their loved ones through a negligent accident. We give you a chance to have your loved one with you again, provided you agree to change your habits."

"But that's impossible," Simon said.

"Seeing is believing, Mr. Kurst. This is truly a second chance to have your lovely wife with you again. Wouldn't you jump at that chance?"

"In a heartbeat," Simon admitted. He thought how convenient that would be. No more worries about what to do with Juniper's body; no living in fear that he would end up in prison. He did not want to be locked up, to have his freedom – and almost certainly, his pride and dignity – taken away. Far beyond anything else, Simon feared his inability to survive in a prison environment. He would be eaten alive, and he knew it.

Not to mention that he would lose the enjoyable lifestyle to which he had become accustomed: his massive paychecks, his Country Club membership, all of his perks, and his very sharp investment team, thanks to his position as Vice President of Operations at Gammo Pharmaceuticals.

"What if I won't do it?" Simon asked.

"If you do not accept the agreement, then all of the photographic evidence in our possession will be released to the authorities. Chances are excellent that you will go to prison. If you decide on that course of action, however, you will still have your money and assets to bargain with, in the event of your incarceration."

"I don't see that as much of a choice," Simon said.

"I must warn you, however. Once you sign this document, there are certain conditions that must be met. If you dishonor those conditions, you will not only lose your wife and freedom. You will lose everything else, as well. All of your physical and nonphysical possessions will revert to Dieter, Worth, and Smite, LLP: this beautiful home, your lovely Ocean City beach house, your three cars, everything in your bank accounts . . . and more."

And more? "So what are these conditions?"

"Keep reading, Mr. Kurst."

Simon looked back down at the paper in his hand. His lips moved as he read. After a couple of minutes, he said, "I can't lay a finger on her."

"That's right. Not so much as a *fingernail*. No punching, no slapping, no choking, no hair pulling. *Ever*. And you can neither neglect her nor abandon this household. Until you die."

Simon could do that. He hoped. He was the epitome of self-control in all aspects of his life – except with Juni. She just had a way of rubbing him the wrong way.

He thought of all the old stories he'd read where people made deals with the Devil. Simon didn't believe in God and the Devil. But this situation was too surreal, too ludicrous, to be anything else. After all, the fact remained – the dead simply did not come back to life. And Smite was too polished, too smooth, and the look in his eyes was dangerously cunning. He looked exactly the way Simon imagined the Devil would look if the Devil actually existed. And what about the sulfur smell that accompanied Smite, and the blue smoke that rose from his person in tendrils? What about the roaring fire that Smite had started in Simon's fireplace – on an intolerably humid summer morning?

Was this even real? He could be going nuts. Maybe Juniper's death had triggered this response. Maybe he was feeling guilty, and it had caused hallucinations. In which case, it wouldn't matter whether or not he signed the agreement.

"Okay," Simon said. "I'll do it."

Smite smiled his wide, white smile. "What a wise decision, Mr. Kurst. I'm sure that, going forward, your new relationship with your wife will be very enlightening." He reached beneath his suit jacket and brought out a pen. "Go ahead and sign on the line. Don't forget the date."

Simon reached out and took the pen. The ink was a dull, brick red against the white paper. It reminded him of the rusty dried blood color in Juni's blonde hair.

As soon as he had finished writing the date next to his signature, a new queasiness in his stomach told him he had just made a very big mistake.

Smite took the paper and handed him another. “This is exactly the same. One is your copy and the other copy is for our records.”

Simon looked the second copy over to make sure that it was the same thing. Then he signed it.

“You may keep the photograph to remind you, Mr. Kurst,” Smite said as he moved toward the door. “And you should be seeing signs of life within the next twenty-four hours. It has been a pleasure doing business with you.” He held out his smoky hand once again for Simon to shake.

For the second time, Simon ignored the gesture. “I wish I could say the same,” he responded.

Smite shrugged and smiled coolly as he stepped outside. “Don’t forget, we’ve got our eyes on you, Mr. Kurst. Good day.”

Simon closed the door firmly behind the departed trespasser and locked it. He pulled the curtain aside at the front window and peered outside, but didn’t see Smite walking up the drive. He didn’t even see Smite’s car. Where had the man gone?

He opened the door, stepped out on to the front porch, and looked around. Smite was nowhere to be seen. There was only a faint blue cloud hanging above the front walk.

He walked the perimeter of the house in his slippers, seeing nothing save the broad expanse of green lawn on that led to the surrounding woods. The gentle summer breeze stirred the treetops; birds chirped and the sun beamed down. There was no sign of Smite. It was as though the man had vanished into thin air.

He could have just slipped into the woods. He could be watching me right now. Simon sighed. What did it matter, anyway?

He gave up and went back inside. After making sure that the door was securely closed and locked, he picked up the bucket beside the hearth and dumped the sand it contained onto Smite's fire, smothering it.

Simon slumped into his recliner beside the fireplace and wiped sweat from his face. This was one of the few times in his adult life that he had felt shaken. He looked at the paper that lay on the sofa beside the photograph Smite had left behind.

Always sharp when it came to contracts and deals, he cursed himself for making such a colossal error. He should never have signed the paper. It was tantamount to a confession. And what if that was really the only photo?

No, Smite had more photos. He didn't know how this photo had been managed, but Simon was sure that Smite hadn't been bluffing. There was no way that Simon was going to risk going to prison. He loved his money and he loved his freedom. But what kind of a price was Simon really going to have to pay to keep them?

And what about Juniper?

For the next couple of hours, Simon's nerves zinged with agitation. He could barely sit still, and his easy chair had lost its friendliness since Smite had occupied it. He forced himself instead to sit back in the corner of his sofa and replay Smite's visit in his mind.

The incident had polarized him into indecision. What should he do next? He had lost his appetite and didn't make breakfast as he'd planned. He feared that at any moment, the police would come knocking at the door.

Every time he thought he heard a noise, he tiptoed up the stairs to check on Juniper, but she still lay in the same position.

He eventually switched on the television. Finding an old horror movie, he lay on the sofa and dozed while he waited for something to happen.

As the day progressed, Simon felt a little better. He shrugged, deciding to adopt a "whatever" attitude. The deed was done and the paper signed. There was nothing he could do about it, now. He wouldn't let his fear of the unknown call a halt to his life. If Juni didn't wake up by tomorrow as Smite had promised, Simon would proceed as originally planned.

He found his appetite close to lunch time, so he made himself a meal. Afterward, he took a shower. Not in the master bath, though; he couldn't stomach the thought of showering with his dead wife lying in the marital bed. He used the shower in the hall bathroom.

Downstairs again and feeling like a new man, Simon watched two more movies and took a pre-dinner nap. When he woke up, he went to the kitchen to prepare himself some dinner.

Thump.

Simon hesitated, listening for a moment. He poured the marinade over the steak, flipped the meat to coat the other side, and snapped the cover closed on the dish. He placed the dish in the refrigerator and closed the door.

Thump! Louder this time. The sound came from upstairs.

Simon grabbed the fireplace poker and slowly climbed the carpeted stairway. He stopped and listened once more at the top of the stairs.

He heard sounds coming from the master bedroom. He crept along the hall, silent in his slippered feet. He stopped at his open bedroom door and surveyed the room.

The bed was empty. The blankets were thrown back, revealing dark red spots dotted here and there and an occasional meandering red drizzle across the sheet.

"You just left me like this."

Simon started at the sound of Juniper's voice.

She stood looking at him from inside the master bathroom. In her hand, she held a wet washcloth. Water ran from the tap into the sink behind her.

"You just left me like this," she repeated. "So many times, over and over. Bloody. Bruised. Injured, broken. You just left me. In the kitchen. In the living room. In the basement." She lifted the washcloth and rubbed at the crusted blood on her face. "You never cleaned me up. You never tried to help me. You never said you were sorry."

Simon just stood there, his mouth partially open, not knowing how to respond.

"I can't believe you did this to me. I can't believe you brought me back! You have to be the most evil, self-absorbed human being on Earth." She paused. "No, scratch that. You aren't even human. You're a monster."

Simon, regaining his composure, retorted, "You ungrateful bitch! I would think you would show a little gratitude after what I've done for you!"

"What you've done *for* me?" Juniper snarled, showing her teeth. "You put me through six years of misery! I kept waiting and waiting for it to be over, for you to finish me off! And there I was, finally at peace, finally at rest, away from you and your cruelty, and you brought me back to this *hellhole!*" She advanced on Simon. The bruises on her face showed in garish relief against her white skin. "Why should I be grateful, after all you've done *to* me, you arrogant little prick?"

Simon took a step back and raised the fireplace poker, shaking it at her. "Now you listen here –"

Juniper cut him off. "No, *you* listen! I know all about that deal you made, Simon. If you want to lose your end of it, be my guest. But if I were you, I would drop – that – poker – *right now!*"

Simon looked at the poker and dropped as though it had burned him. "H-how do you –"

"How do I know? *Hello,* dead woman in the house!" She stepped forward, grabbed the poker, and brandished it in front of her. "Floating all over the place, watching you being an idiot!" Juniper laughed, a high-pitched cackle that made Simon's neck hair stand up and sent chills down his spine. "Boy, did *you* get screwed over!"

"What?"

"I'm dead, you fool! I haven't been brought back to life! I'm still *dead!*"

Simon stared at her. "But that's not right. The agreement clearly stated that you would be returned 'as living'. And here you are!"

"That's right, Simon. 'As living.' Not *alive!* My soul and my body are *permanently separated!* You can't stuff a soul back into a dead body. It's like trying to put toothpaste back into the tube, or an egg back into its shell. I have no working bodily functions."

"Then how are you standing there and walking and talking?"

"*I* don't know! I didn't make the deal. Maybe it's *maagiiiic.*" She made her voice low and mysterious, drawing out the word.

Simon let out his breath in one big "whoosh".

"You made a deal to bring me back to keep your ass out of prison. And you thought I would go back to being your servant – and personal punching bag – the way I've been for the past six years, ever since I married you." She shook the poker at him. "Let me tell *you* something, *mister!* You want to stay out of prison? You want to keep your cash, your clothes, your house, your cars, your gold cufflinks, and your membership at the country club? You better not even *think* about touching me, because *those* days are over. I'm not your punching bag anymore." She held the fireplace poker back over her shoulder like a baseball bat. She swung it at his head. It made a humming sound as it cut through the air. He winced, closed his eyes, and raised his arms defensively in front of him.

Juniper halted her motion just short of Simon's ear. "You'd better remember that." She turned and went back into the bathroom, where the tap was still running. She leaned the poker against the wall beside the sink, shut the tap off and looked up. Her eyes met Simon's in the mirror. "I'm going to take a shower now and clean up this mess you made. When I come downstairs, you'd better have some dinner sitting on the table, waiting for me."

Simon stood and stared at her.

She smiled. "Get to it! *Now!*"

Not knowing what else to do, Simon got to it.

In the kitchen, he cursed to himself resentfully and stared at the steak he had intended to make for his dinner. Well, he supposed he could split it with Juniper. It was big enough.

Damn! What am I going to do? This is not *what I signed up for.* And then a nagging voice in the back of his mind said, *Yes, yes you did. You just didn't know it.*

This Juniper wasn't the Juniper he knew. *His* Juniper was quiet, meek, and docile. Death had changed her, and not for the better.

And whose fault is that? The voice interjected. He ignored it.

Wasn't staying out of prison worth a little humiliation? And keeping all of his worldly possessions? It wasn't like he was losing face in front of his colleagues or in the public eye. This was a private matter between him and Juniper. No one else knew except for Andrew Smite and his supposed "partners". So she had transformed into a bitch. He'd dealt with bitches before.

He busied himself making dinner. When Juniper came downstairs, fireplace poker in hand, her hot meal was sitting on the table, just as she'd commanded.

She looked at the food sitting on the table and said, "What did you do, cook it in a bonfire?"

Indeed, a telltale smoky haze drifted from the kitchen doorway.

"No, it's broiled. It's just a little well done," Simon said, irritated. What did she expect? He hadn't cooked a steak dinner in years.

"I don't think it looks 'well done' at all. It looks very poorly done. Throw it away and then clean up whatever mess you made in the kitchen."

"You aren't going to eat?"

"Dead people don't eat, you moron."

"Then why did you tell me to make you dinner?"

"Because I *could,* that's why." Juniper looked at the second place setting on the dining room table. "And what is this?"

"That's *my* plate."

"Did I tell you to make *yourself* dinner? No, I don't think I did." With one motion, she swiped his plate off of the table. Baked potato and rice splattered across the hardwood, and the plate spun on its edge for a few seconds before it settled in place. She did the same with her own plate.

"Hey!" Simon protested. "What the hell? I paid for that food. That was a waste of perfectly good food!"

"Oh really? Well, guess what. You killing me? *That* was a waste of a perfectly good *life.* Don't you think? Now, clean up this mess, and then clean the kitchen, like I told you to. And when you're done with that, you can make my bed with clean sheets. Then maybe you can have a bowl of cereal or something." She raised the fireplace poker menacingly.

Simon, fuming, fought to keep his emotion under control. He wanted to grab Juniper, slam her into the wall, shake her, choke her, throw her on the floor and stomp her face. The new voice, which apparently must be his conscience (*who knew I even had one of those?*) spoke up: *That's how you ended up in this situation in the first place. Moron.*

His face red, he stood there and glared at her, grinding his teeth. A tic jumped in his left cheek. A vein stood out in his forehead.

He looked at the poker in her hand. "Yes, dearest," he said.

Juniper smiled a grotesque smile, then turned and went to the living room. He heard the television click on.

For the first time since his wife had died, Simon noticed that two of her teeth were missing.

When Monday morning arrived, Simon couldn't get ready for work fast enough. He showered and dressed with enthusiasm, eager to escape the house, which now felt like a prison.

Overnight, he had become Juniper's servant. She made him sleep in one of the guest bedrooms, which didn't bother him; what *did* bother him were the never ending demands she made upon him.

Like preparing meal after meal that she would not eat; meals that she wouldn't allow *him* to eat. Every time she came to the table she commented derisively and made him throw the food away. She watched him to make sure he threw it in the trash. She designated exactly what he was to eat and when he was allowed to eat it.

By Sunday evening, he had scrubbed both bathrooms twice, done the laundry, hauled in wood for the fireplace, mowed the lawn, cleaned out the refrigerator, and had started cleaning the basement.

Whenever he protested, she nudged him with the fireplace poker. She'd swung it at him a few times, but she hadn't hit him with it. Yet.

Juniper met Simon at the bottom of the stairs. "Don't you look handsome," she said. "Off to work?"

Simon nodded.

"I have really good news for you honey. You get a free week off from work! You've been working so hard. You really deserve a vacation. And besides . . . don't you remember there's a special day coming up this week?"

"No. And I have some really important meetings scheduled this week. I can't take any time off."

"Oh, sure you can! Our anniversary is this week. I called your office and arranged everything. Your assistant will be standing in for you."

Simon's heart started beating in his ears. The noise was thunderous. His lips practically disappeared in a thin line that cut across his face. He was not amused. "Juniper, you are interfering with my livelihood. You're really crossing the line here, going way too far."

"Oh, really." It was a statement, not a question. "Well, gee, Mr. Important, do you think *you* went a little too far when you did this?" She moved her hair back away from her face and showed him her right ear, from which the entire earlobe was missing. "Or how about *this*?" She held up her arm. It was scarred all the way from wrist to elbow with discolored and wrinkled patches. "You had a *good* fire burning that night, didn't you? What about *this*?" She stuck her pinky finger in the air. The finger was permanently bent out from her hand at an extremely awkward angle. "Or how about these?" She smiled and pointed to the gaps in her lower jaw where two teeth were missing.

"Welcome to *my* world, *hubby*," she hissed. "What you've had to do doesn't even come *close* to how it felt to be me. How about I repay you with a few disfigurements of your own?"

"How *dare* you threaten me!"

"How dare I? *How dare I*? Obviously you need reminding that I'm the woman that you *killed*, your *wife*, no less, the same wife that you promised to love, cherish, and protect until death do us part. I think you've been a little remiss with your vows. If you had done what you had promised, you wouldn't be in this situation. Speaking of which, how would you like a quick trip to prison tonight? Maybe you should think about *that*." She smacked him on the arm with the poker, hard enough to sting, but not hard enough to bruise him.

Simon remained silent. He was sick of thinking about this "situation". He was sick of Juniper reminding him of this "situation" each day, every chance she had.

He quietly completed every task Juniper demanded of him, while he fumed inside. He carefully prepared complicated recipes and threw them away, while his diet consisted of hot dogs, canned pasta, and cereal. Every day he vacuumed all of the carpets, swept and polished the hardwood, scrubbed both bathrooms and the kitchen, and dusted the furniture. Then there were additional chores: cutting firewood, cleaning the attic, washing the clothes, whatever Juniper could think of.

The chores weren't easy for Simon. He'd been sitting behind a desk for the past eleven years. The most strenuous lifting he had done was to lift pens for signing contracts and checks. During the first couple of days, his body grew stiff and sore from the physical activity to which his body was unaccustomed.

He grew angrier with each passing day, but Juniper kept him in check with the damned fireplace poker. Just enough to remind him of the agreement he had signed, and of the photograph depicting evidence of his guilt.

He reflected upon his abrupt lack of control. He had always controlled every part of his life: work, home, Juniper, his acquaintances. His control had been wrested from him, and he didn't like it one bit. He wracked his brain, following his thoughts in circles, trying to find a way out of this "situation", but he couldn't see any way out, other than to turn himself in and confess. And he wasn't going to do that.

Hell, he couldn't even just leave Juniper. He couldn't abandon the house. This was *his* house, damn it! He'd had it designed and built for him long before Juni had come in to his life. Everything in it was *his*. He wasn't about to relinquish any of his possessions, all of the fortune he had worked so hard to amass. Juni wasn't entitled to a dime. But if he skipped out on her, he would lose it all.

It's just not fair! The thought was petulant, like an argumentative child.

The other voice, more faint, spoke up: *But this is the choice you made.*

He couldn't deny it.

He did the best he could, despite the circumstances. He hoped that if he performed the tasks well, Juniper's rage would mellow, and maybe she would relent and he might be let out of the contract.

At least she stayed out of his way, most of the time. She emerged from her bedroom just long enough to give orders, to check that he had done the tasks she'd assigned to him, and to check the food he prepared. Otherwise, she stayed shut in . . . except when he heard her creaking around the dark house in the small hours of the morning. Simon stayed in his room during her nocturnal wanderings. Juniper was damned *creepy*. She scared him.

Simon wanted to kill his wife – again. *You can't kill what's already dead*, he thought. There were so many things he wanted to do to her from which he would derive satisfaction: break all of her fingers. Break her ribs and smash in her skull with a hammer. Beat her down and kick her until her ribs were broken.

But he couldn't touch a hair on Juniper's head. Not that there would be anything left to touch on her decomposing scalp, in a few weeks.

One of the things he was finding as he cleaned the house each day was Juniper's hair. At first he found strands here and there. More recently, he had been finding small, honey colored clumps, sometimes with skin attached. They smelled like rot. Whenever Simon came across one of these treats, he wrinkled his nose and got the gloves. He wouldn't touch the stuff with his bare hands.

He was also finding what seemed to be flakes of skin. These were becoming larger and more prevalent as the days passed. The large ones were more like gooey chunks. They stank so bad he wanted to vomit into the trash as he tossed them away.

Juni's rotting, road-kill smell was permeating Simon's entire house. The ripe, foul odor grew stronger with each passing day.

On the brief occasions when she showed her face, Simon noticed that she looked worse and worse. The skin of her face appeared as though it was melting. He could see parts of her graying flesh hanging off here and there in clumps and small shreds, and her teeth and parts of her jawbone jutted out, unprotected. Half of her scalp was completely gone, revealing the dirty looking parts of her skull beneath. She hadn't changed her clothing in days. Filthy with her decomposition, the shirt and jeans hung off of her skeletal frame.

It made his skin crawl with disgust.

It cheered Simon to think that maybe Juni would simply decay and fall apart, and he would be free again.

He could just wait her out. But how long would that take? She was repulsive. He wasn't sure just how much more of this he could stand.

And he couldn't help but feel apprehensive about what was to come the day of their anniversary.

* * *

He was on edge that whole day; Friday, July 28th. He waited and waited, but he barely saw Juniper that day. He began to believe that, in her crumbling state, she had forgotten about the date.

He began to breathe a little easier as time wore on and the hour became later and later. Finally, he went to bed.

His worst fears were realized when, shortly before midnight, he woke to the sound of the bed springs creaking as his dead wife slid beneath the blankets beside him. The stench was ungodly.

She moved close to him and draped a bony arm across his chest. "Don't you remember our special day? It's our anniversary! Today was the day that you put the ring on my finger and we both said, 'I do'. We said our vows. But you've been neglecting me, hubby. That's against the rules. Tsk, tsk, tsk. What do you say, baby? Let's celebrate our anniversary with some old-fashioned lovin'." Her voice gurgled and her fetid breath drifted up to his face.

Simon gagged and retched. Moaning, he pushed her arm away and threw the blankets aside. He stumbled out of the room.

Behind him, Juniper laughed, a low, gurgling, husky noise. "Aww, come on now, hubby! Now you're hurting my feelings!" She called after him.

Never! Never, never, never, never, never!

He locked himself in his office.

There was still one thing he had control of.

* * *

Juniper slunk down the stairs to check on him about a half hour later. She rapped on the door of his office. “Simon,” she called in her gurgling voice.

Silence.

She called out and knocked again. When there was still no response, she pulled on a pair of latex disposable gloves she had grabbed from the kitchen.

Fishing a key from her pocket, Juniper unlocked the office door. When she found her husband dangling by his neck from the central beam in the exposed ceiling, she ran upstairs to shower and clean herself up.

Afterward, she donned a fresh pair of latex gloves before rummaging through her dead husband’s pockets, dropping the key into one of them when she was finished.

Juniper then searched the room, careful to leave everything exactly as she had found it, with the exception of the contract Simon had signed with Smite, along with the telltale photograph. These she confiscated before she exited the room, closing the door securely behind her. She made sure it was locked, then busied herself with a meticulous cleaning of the house, searching for any clue her husband might have left regarding the incidents that had occurred during the past few days. As she cleaned, she gathered up the three decomposing rats that she had planted through the house. She tossed them out into the woods.

Satisfied with her cleanup, Simon Kurst’s lovely young wife climbed between the freshly changed sheets of the marital bed and slept soundly.

In the morning, Juniper dialed 911.

* * *

Twelve months later in Ocean City, Maryland, a slender, attractive woman in her late twenties sat on her rear deck, facing the beach and the ocean beyond. Her honey colored hair shone brightly in the early morning sun.

The woman wore a comfortable fleece-lined sweat suit against the chilly, damp breeze that blew in off of the rolling surf. She warmed her hands around her morning cup of coffee as she perused the pages of the daily newspaper.

A figure appeared at the north end of the beach. As it approached she could see that it was that of a tall man, whose white polo shirt and khaki shorts stood out against his deep tan. His silvery-gray hair was combed impeccably back from his forehead, and he carried a brown briefcase.

The woman jumped up and waved excitedly. "Uncle Drew! You're so early!"

"I hope you don't mind," Andrew James said, climbing the steps to Juniper's deck. He hugged her briefly and bent to give her a peck on the cheek.

"Of course I don't mind, Uncle Drew! I don't care what time of day it is. I love to see you! Why don't you have a seat?"

He folded himself into one of her deck chairs while Juniper poured him a cup from the ceramic pot on the table. "Thank you, my dear," Drew said, adding sugar and cream from the containers Juniper had set out.

"It's so nice to see you again!" Juniper dropped comfortably into her chair.

"And you." Drew sipped his coffee. "You look lovely this morning. Single life has been good for you. And safely ensconced in the beach house. You did well."

"I never would have any of this without your help. You saved my life!"

"Ah, Cinderella turned Princess. All is now as it should be. And I'm so glad that we were able to be of assistance."

"The Second Skin was unbelievable! I was so worried that it wouldn't work, but Simon didn't have a clue! It even made my skin feel cold and stiff. What was in that?"

"We're always trying new products in this modern age of theater," her guest said proudly. "I couldn't tell you exactly what it's made of. I believe it is oil-based. You saw how it worked. It's a petroleum-jelly like substance that hardens into a thin, skin-like covering. It's really just a new, lightweight form of stage makeup. The insulating and 'sound-proofing' properties just happened to be additional characteristics that the developer discovered, quite by accident."

Juniper shook her head. "I still can't believe the whole thing worked. Simon never believed in the supernatural. You must have been quite convincing."

"I've been in drama for a very long time, my dear, and I am privy to tricks and effects that not every actor knows about. I pulled out all of the stops for you. Your father would have murdered that man in cold blood, had he known what ill fortune had befallen you." He shook his head, then flashed a bright white smile. "*You* must have been *much* more convincing. After all, you had to play your part for several days. It must have been so difficult to take the makeup off and re-apply it, every day. It's a wonder you weren't discovered."

"Oh, no, I never took it off. I just put more on. The more I left it, the worse I looked." She wrinkled her face and shuddered. "The dead rats were the worst, though."

Drew looked at her inquisitively. "Dead rats?"

Juniper smiled and waved it away. "Never mind, it isn't important. I'm just glad to be sitting here with you."

"And I, with you. Still, I would have loved to have been there for your performance. The Actors Guild would have been so proud!"

"The Actors Guild! Hold on a second, Uncle Drew. Before I forget, I have something for you." Juniper stood and went through the sliding glass door into the house. She returned with two pieces of paper. "Five thousand to the Baker City Actors Guild, and seventeen thousand to James, Jenson, and Collins. That should settle us up. Thank you so much for representing me and helping with my late husband's estate."

Drew took the checks and deposited them into a pocket of his briefcase. "Few could be more deserving of the help than you."

"Well, if you and the Actors Guild hadn't sent me that postcard, I doubt I would be here, today. And you – well, of course Simon tried to disinherit me. Thanks to you, he wasn't allowed to leave me destitute."

"You are very kind, my dear." Smite took a last sip of his coffee and stood. "I have a nine-thirty appointment, so I must be off. I will be flying home tomorrow afternoon." He hesitated. "But before I leave, I must ask you . . . would you consider re-joining the troupe and pursuing your acting career again?"

Juniper smiled, standing to take her uncle's proffered hand. "I would consider it."

"Why don't I collect you for dinner this evening, then? A couple of the troupe members are actually here in town with me. I'm sure that they would love to reunite with you. We can have a good conversation."

"That would be wonderful."

Drew paused for a moment. "I just have one question. How did you know that your husband would kill himself?"

Juniper shook her head and raised her hands helplessly. "I didn't. That was never my intention. I just wanted to drive him a little crazy for a while and show him how it felt to be treated the way he treated me."

"Interesting." Drew stepped forward and enfolded Juniper in his long arms. "Until this evening, Mrs. Kurst. I will call on you around seven o'clock."

Juniper laughed. "Until then. And it's Ms. Henry, now."

Drew chuckled and descended her back steps. "Very well then, Ms. Henry."

"See you later, Uncle Drew!" Juniper waved to him as he made his way across the sand.

COOKOUT AT THE ZEIKS'

Eight year-old Gordie Zeik wolfed down his after-school milk and cookies and yelled, "I'm gonna go play in my room!"

"Okay, Gordie," his mother, Maryann, called back. "You know where I am if you need me!"

"'Kay."

Gordie ran off to his room, eager to play with the new race track he'd gotten for Christmas. But first, he needed to greet his hamster, Harry P.

"Hi, Harry P!" He peered into the hamster cage. He didn't see his fluffy little brown-and-white pet. Maybe he was in the half-chewed toilet paper roll, or buried beneath the cardboard chips and aspen bedding.

"Harry P?"

Gordie noticed that the cage door was open. He stared at it for a moment, then reached his hand inside the opening and felt around in the bedding. He picked up the empty toilet paper roll. Harry P was gone.

"Harry P!" Gordie called. He searched the shelf upon which the cage sat. He dropped to the floor and looked under the bed. Calling the hamster's name, he crawled along the carpet, searching beneath all of the furniture and in the corners of his room. He picked up his dirty socks, undershorts, and pajamas, shaking them out. He searched his closet.

No Harry P.

Panicking, Gordie ran to his mom's office, knocked on the door and opened it. "Mom, I can't find Harry P!"

Maryann turned away from the computer. "What?"

"Harry P is gone! He's not in his cage and he's not in my room!" Tears slid down the boy's freckled cheeks.

"Oh, honey!" Maryann reached out for Gordie and gathered him to her in a big hug. "Stay calm. I'll help you look again."

Gordie grabbed her hand and pulled her into his room. He pointed at the empty cage. "See?"

"What happened? Did he escape while you were playing with him?"

"No, Mom, the door was open when I came in, and Harry P was already gone!"

"Really?" Maryann frowned. She reached into Harry P's cage and dug through the aspen chips as Gordie had done. "Hmm. Let's look around your room again."

They searched Gordie's room, but still didn't find Harry P.

"Maybe he got out of your room and he's in the house somewhere. Or maybe Nathan took him out to play," she suggested. "Go ask your brother. I'll look in the living room."

Gordie did as she instructed and ran upstairs to get Nate. He knocked on his brother's door. After a moment, he heard a spraying noise like his mom's bathroom cleaner.

"Who is it?" Nate's voice was muffled behind the door.

"It's me. Have you seen Harry P? He's gone!"

Nate opened the door. He wore only pajama bottoms, and his hair was tousled. A sweet, weird smell came wafting out of his room, mixed with the smell of oranges.

"Now, what's going on?"

Gordie nearly jumped up and down with frustration. "Harry P is gone! Did you play with him? Have you seen him?"

"No," Nate said, yawning. "I've been in bed all day."

Gordie's face started to crumple. "But I'll help you look for him, little bro," Nate said quickly, landing a mock punch on Gordie's shoulder. "Hold on a sec."

He shut the door and emerged a moment later after donning his slippers and robe.

Maryann and the boys scoured the house, searching beneath and behind the furniture, in the laundry, in cupboards and closets. Their search came up empty.

Gordie began to cry again.

Maryann knelt down and put her hands on his shoulders. "Gordie, Harry P is tiny and can fit into very small spaces. Chances are he's found a little hiding place somewhere and he's sleeping. He can't have gone far. He has to be in the house *somewhere*. He'll turn up eventually."

"Mom's right," Nate assured him. "It'll be okay."

"What if it isn't?" Gordie sobbed.

"It *will* be," Maryann said firmly. "But right now, I need to make dinner, and you still have homework to do. You have to keep going even when you're sad."

"Yeah, Gordie. Tell you what. Why don't I help you with your homework?" Nate offered.

Gordie nodded reluctantly, his chest still heaving.

"Let's get you some tissues first."

Maryann smiled gratefully at Nate and went to the kitchen to prepare dinner.

By bedtime, Harry P still hadn't shown up. Gordie tossed and turned in his bed for a while before finally falling into a fitful sleep.

He dreamed of a bonfire and the smell of barbeque.

The next morning, after Maryann saw a very sad Gordie off on the school bus, she went to his room. She stood in his doorway and stared at Harry P's cage, frowning. After a moment or two, she became aware of a smell – a smell like roasted meat . . . and the faint odor of wood smoke.

She walked slowly around the room, sniffing the air, trying to identify the source of the smell. She knelt down at the foot of the bed and lifted the comforter to look beneath.

"What the . . . ?"

In the morning sunlight that streamed between Gordie's open curtains and made its way beneath his bed, she saw one of his large wooden blocks. On top of this was a small pile of ash, as though from a fire. Standing above the pile of ash was a tiny frame made of various toy parts; it resembled a spit for roasting meat over a fire. She reached out and touched the wooden block. Though the ashes were cold, the block was warm. Then she saw the little pile of bones.

"Oh, fudge," she said softly.

Next to the pile of bones was a piece of brown cloth. She hooked it with the tip of her finger and pulled it out from beneath the bed. She held it up and examined it.

It was a piece of clothing, a tunic of some kind. Maryann wrinkled her nose; the thing smelled rancid. It was covered with dirt and dark stains that looked fresh. When she touched the stains, they felt damp. Her fingers came away red.

Blood?

She went upstairs and rousted her older son from his bed. "Nathan, there's something I want you to see."

"It isn't more college brochures, is it? Because-"

Maryann gave him a look. "No, Nathan, this is more immediate. I think it has to do with Harry P."

"Oh."

They went to Gordie's room, where Maryann had him look under the bed.

"There's bones under there," Nate said, looking up at her. "It smells like a pig roast. And it looks like there was a fire. Jesus, Mom, do you think that's Harry P?"

"Unfortunately, I do. The bones look like those of a tiny animal."

"I wonder why the smoke detectors didn't go off," Nate said. "We're lucky Gordie's bed didn't catch on fire." He paused for a moment. "Mom . . . do you think *he* did this?"

His mother gave him another look. "He's an eight year-old boy. I don't think he would kill and eat his own pet. You saw how heartbroken he was."

Nate shrugged. "Stranger things have happened."

"Look at this." Maryann held up the bloodstained tunic.

He stared. "What is it?"

"I have no idea." Silence filled the room as he absorbed the weight of her statement.

"Oh, crap."

"You said it."

"What do we do?"

"First, I'm making a fresh pot of coffee. Then we need to discuss this. In the living room."

* * *

Maryann scraped a dab of peanut butter into the back of each of the two small box-style mousetraps. She had chosen these traps, rather than spring traps, because they were humane and wouldn't kill or injure the rodent, but would contain it. She wouldn't be able to forgive herself if Harry P was alive and running loose around the house and she killed or hurt the hamster in a spring trap.

"What now?" Nate asked.

"We go about our business."

They left everything in Gordie's room exactly the way they had found it that morning. Maryann had replaced the tunic beside the pile of bones under the bed, hoping that its disturbance would go unnoticed.

"Do you really think it will come back?"

"I don't know. But if you found a meal somewhere for free, wouldn't you be tempted to go back and try again?"

"Yeah, I guess so." He switched on the television, setting the volume slightly lower than usual, and settled himself in the recliner.

Maryann smiled tightly and went to the kitchen to do the breakfast dishes, hoping that it wouldn't take too long to catch the thing, whatever it was.

She moved around the house, doing daily chores, while Nate watched movies. Eventually she brought him a new stack of college brochures.

"Oh, Mom," he groaned.

"Well, you've got to do *something*."

"Can't I just get a job as a gas station attendant?"

"Sweetheart, you can get a job anywhere you want, as long as you're doing something productive."

"Fine," Nate sighed. He rifled through the stack of brochures.

Maryann went into Gordie's room and gathered his dirty clothes from the floor. Everything was quiet and appeared undisturbed.

As she was about to leave the room, Maryann thought she heard something. She turned and paused in the doorway.

She heard the sound again. It came from the direction of Gordie's toy box.

She held her breath and watched intently. She saw Gordie's little white cash register at the top of the untidy pile. Just beneath it were his remote control truck and his old animatronic bear.

The noise continued. It sounded the same way it did when Gordie was looking through his toy box for something to play with: things being pushed aside, other things tumbling down to take their place.

Did the bear just move? She wasn't sure.

Wait . . . yes, the bear seemed to be moving – just a tiny bit, barely enough for the motion to be detectable.

She began to feel just a little afraid. *Maybe it's nothing,* she thought. *Maybe the bear's switch just got knocked, and the bear turned on.*

The feeling in the pit of her stomach told her it was more than that. She didn't want to call for Nate, yet. If it was Gordie's visitor from the night before, she didn't want to tip it off and send it back into hiding. She wanted to catch it and *get rid of it.*

Maryann stared with fascinated apprehension as the bear heaved upward, dislodging the cash register from the top of the pile of toys. She jumped when it flipped over and fell to the floor with a crash and a *ding!* as the drawer popped open.

A little brown and white head, with tiny round ears and long, white whiskers, popped up from among the toys. It sniffed the air for a second; then it continued to root around in the toy box.

Maryann smiled in wonder and relief. *Harry P!* But even as she watched, her heart sank, and she knew it wasn't so.

She realized that whatever this creature was, it was wearing Harry P's skin, head and all. *Oh my God, it skinned Gordie's hamster!*

Beneath Harry P's stolen skin, the thing was brown. It had a wrinkled leathery face, and its two arms and the front of its body were covered in short brown fur. The skin of its wrinkly brown hands matched its face. It stood upright on two legs, which were also covered in brown fur.

Maryann felt a surge of disgust as she watched the tiny creature tip its head back and sniff again. It stared over at Harry P's cage, hoping to catch the scent of its next potential meal.

It eagerly clambered over the toys, using all fours, and dropped down to the carpet. It reached up to the lowest shelf of Gordie's bookcase and hauled itself up.

Maryann waited until it had reached the top shelf before she said loudly, "Oh, no you don't, you little monster!"

It turned and saw her. It threw its head back and let out a high pitched screech, exposing rows of neat little razor-sharp teeth.

It launched itself off the shelf and landed on the toy box. It grabbed something from the pile of toys, jumped on the bed, and leaped at Maryann, screeching all the way.

"Mom!" She heard Nate's voice behind her in the hall.

Maryann snapped one arm out in front of her and snatched the six-inch tall creature out of the air with her left hand, closing her fist around it firmly. She screamed as sharp pain lanced through her palm. Opening her fingers, she realized that the thing held the tiny plastic sword from Gordie's Swashbuckling Pirate Play Set. She had closed her hand around the blade, and the creature had pulled it against her palm at such an angle that it had sliced her palm open. Blood ran freely from the wound. She switched hands, making sure that the sword was positioned above her enclosed fingers.

Nate stood in the door as and stared in horror as the scene unfolded. The creature struggled in his mother's hand. It raised the sword and plunged the blade repeatedly into her hand as she winced in pain.

"*What do I do, what do I do?!*" He cried.

"*Get the sword, get the sword!*"

Nate stepped forward and wrestled briefly with the creature, trying to grasp the tiny sword with his fingertips. He finally managed to wrench the sword away.

"Go get a cold, wet towel!"

When Nathan stayed rooted to the spot, transfixed, Maryann shouted, "Nathan, *go!*"

He started, then ran upstairs to the bathroom and grabbed the towel off the rack and turned on the "Cold" tap in the sink. As he ran water over the towel he heard his mother screaming.

"You ate Harry P! That's my child's pet, you little *bipedal rat thing!*"

Leaving the water running in the sink, Nate raced down the stairs.

"Put the towel over it! Quick!"

Nate threw the cold, dripping towel over the thing's head. Even as Maryann screamed at him to wrap the creature up, he was swaddling the writhing creature, rendering it immobile.

Maryann gasped, sweat running in rivulets down her face. Her hands dripped blood.

"Mom, are you okay?" Nate looked as though he was going to cry.

"I'm okay, I'm okay, see? All I need to do is wash my hands and wrap them up, and I'll be fine. Could you help me?"

The two of them headed up to the bathroom, Nate still hanging on to the struggling thing in the towel.

Maryann rinsed her trembling hands in the cold water Nate had left running. There were several nasty puncture marks in the webbing between the thumb and forefinger of one hand, the other had one single slash across the palm. There were teeth marks in several places where the creature had bitten her.

Nate held the bottle of peroxide firmly in one hand while Maryann turned the cap. She held her hands over the sink and he dumped the peroxide liberally on them. She inhaled through her teeth at the stinging.

"What is this thing, Mom?" Nate asked.

"I don't know. It came out of Gordie's toy box."

"What are we going to do with it?"

"I'd love to kill the thing, but we're going to call Animal Control and let them deal with it, because I have no other ideas."

Nate found some gauze and a couple of rolled bandages. He and Maryann worked together to get her hands wrapped.

When the Animal Control officers arrived, they managed to get the screeching creature into a cage.

"You'd better make sure that cage door is chained up so that it can't get out. Because I can almost promise you that it will figure out that simple slide latch. And it's mean!"

"Where did you find it?" Asked Officer Patel, the younger of the two responders. He didn't look much older than Nate.

"It came out of my younger son's toy box," Maryann told them. She led them to Gordie's room and showed them the spit, the ashes, the pile of bones, and the tunic under Gordie's bed.

"That thing roasted my little boy's hamster on that spit and ate it while he was sleeping in his bed last night," she said "Then it attacked me when it came sneaking out looking for more. Have you guys ever seen something like this before?"

The two men looked at each other. Officer Dillard, the elder and stouter of the two, said, "No ma'am. I can't recall ever seeing anything like this. The thing is intelligent enough to use tools, cook, *and* make clothing?" He shook his head and looked at Maryann's bandaged hands. "I think you'd better go to the hospital and get those looked at, just in case. You might even consider a rabies shot," he said. "Do you know where this thing came from, in the first place? You got a basement? Have you seen any more?"

"Yes, we have a basement," Maryann said. "Do you really think there might be more than one?"

"We don't know how many there are. This is something new and different, to us, anyway. Another agency may have come across this; we're going to try to find out. I think it would be a good idea to get hold of a wildlife management agency and have your place swept for more of these critters. With something as aggressive as this, it's better to be safe than sorry." He glanced at the thing in the cage. It rattled the wire bars, emitting short shrieks, sounding like an angry bird. "Do you and your kids have a place you could stay for a couple of days?"

Maryann gave Nate a troubled look. "I guess we could probably stay at Aunt Janice's," she said.

"Cool!" Nate exclaimed.

"Do you really think this is serious enough to warrant us leaving?"

"Like I said, ma'am, in this case, I think we should be cautious. At least until we can make sure the property is clear."

Maryann sighed. "Okay, we'd better pack some clothes for a couple of days. Nate, dial the phone for me, would you? You'll have to hold it for me, too."

Nate laughed a little and she gave him a look. "I know it isn't funny, Mom, but it is, just a little."

Maryann turned back to the officers. "We'll get Gordie off the bus and then we'll be going."

"We'll give you a call when we set up a meeting with wildlife management," Officer Dillard said. "Will you be available to let us in?"

"I'll have Nathan unlock the door for you. Just let me know."

Maryann and Nate met Gordie at the school bus, and they all piled into the car.

"Where are we going, guys? Hey, did you find Harry P?" Gordie asked.

"We're going to Aunt Janice's to stay for a couple of days," Maryann said. "And no, we didn't find Harry P, yet. I'm sorry."

His face fell. "What if we never find him?"

"Well, it looks like he escaped. He's probably living it up by now, chewing his way through a cereal box in the cupboard. There are enough warm and cozy places for him to hide in the house. He's probably found a place to make a nice nest."

"If we don't find him, I'm going to miss him. I love him so much!" Gordie's voice sounded tearful.

"I know, Gordie, and I really am sorry that we lost him," Maryann said. "We all love him, and we'll miss him, too. Maybe we can get you a new pet."

Gordie's face brightened for the first time in days. "Can I have a guinea pig?"

Nate drove them to Janice's where they dropped Gordie off, and then took his mother to the hospital to have her hands checked.

Animal Control scheduled a sweep of the Zeik property the next morning.

Meanwhile, in a maze of countless subterranean tunnels far beneath the basement floor, hundreds of six-inch tall creatures grew restless as they waited for their scout to return.

JOY

Lauren drove down Blackberry Lane, slowing to steer her car carefully around the big moving van parked on the right side of the street in front of the dilapidated house that stood opposite her own residence. She edged forward, her view of the sidewalk obstructed by the van. She saw the ball first: a big yellow beach ball adorned with a single red stripe and the cartoon face of a dark-skinned girl sporting a pageboy haircut and a backpack. Lauren stepped on the brake as the ball bounced slowly into the street, and she waited patiently for the ball's owner, a little girl in a dirt-streaked pink sundress, to retrieve it. The girl looked fearfully at Lauren, who smiled and waved at her.

"*Lainie*!" A high-pitched voice screeched. Lauren winced as the unpleasant sound reached through her open car windows. The voice was followed by a bony, hatchet-faced woman, who glared at Lauren as she grabbed the little girl's arm and yanked her roughly to the curb. Lauren waited for a few seconds after the two had disappeared behind the van before she proceeded the last few feet to her driveway on the left.

Pulling in, Lauren noticed her neighbor, Rita Williams, standing on her front porch. Her red-lipsticked mouth wearing a thin grimace, Rita jerked her head toward the house across the street, then shook her head, rolling her eyes. She had apparently seen the brief encounter. *Actually, she's probably been watching the new neighbors move in all day long*, Lauren thought.

She smiled as she exited the car. "Hey, Rita, what's happening?" she called over.

Rita returned her smile, her plump face crinkling up in a pleasant web of lines and wrinkles. "Why don't you come over for a glass of iced tea when you get settled? I'll give you the gossip." She winked at Lauren, who laughed.

"Sure," she said. "Let me get Mop settled and I'll be over."

At the door, she could see her daughter's English shepherd jumping up and down on the other side of the window. She unlocked her door and pushed it open. "Down, down!" She shouted, laughing. Mop stood on her hind feet, placed his paws on Lauren's shoulders, and licked her face.

Lauren kicked off her pumps, roughed up Mop's fur, and hugged his sturdy, warm, wriggling body. She ran down the hall to the kitchen in her stocking feet; Mop chased her joyfully. Knowing the drill, he launched himself through the back door when Lauren held it open for him. She propped the screen door so that Mop could come in through his doggie door when he was done with his run around the fenced-in back yard.

Meanwhile, Lauren ran upstairs to change out of her skirt and blouse into a comfortable pair of jeans and a t-shirt. She stopped to blow a kiss to the photograph of Michael and Allie, then grabbed Rita's plate from her dish drainer and headed next door.

"Here's your plate back! Thanks so much for the cookies, they were awesome!"

The older woman took the plate. "You're so welcome, dear! Have a seat, I've poured you a glass of iced tea."

"Thanks!" Lauren dropped into one of Rita's porch chairs and stretched her legs, propping her sneakered feet up on the porch railing. She turned her head to check on Mop in her back yard. He was on his back, squirming and wriggling on the lush green grass. She closed her eyes and breathed deeply, inhaling the fresh autumn air. It was good to be out of work, sitting outside in the warmth of the September day. The porch roof provided relief from the bright sunshine.

Hearing the sound of an approaching vehicle, Lauren looked down the road. The posted speed limit on that part of Blackberry Lane was 30 mph, but the dark blue car moving toward her was going substantially faster. It zoomed past, swerving around the white moving van.

"Jeez," Lauren said, shaking her head.

"What's that?" The screen door slammed as Rita returned from taking the plate inside.

"The traffic on this road is stupid. They completely ignore the speed zone. Someday, someone's really going to get hurt."

"Oh, I know. We need a yellow blinking light at each end to help remind people to slow down. Whew, it's a lovely day, isn't it? It is just a little hot for me, though." Rita lowered her powder-green polyester-clad behind into the other chair and fanned herself with that day's newspaper. She held her foggy glass of iced tea against her forehead, then took a swig from it, leaving a red lip-print behind. "How's Lauren today?"

Lauren shrugged. "Eh. You know. You been over yet?" She nodded at the ramshackle brown house across the street.

"No, I'm waiting a day or two. Let them get settled in a little, first. Though from what I've seen, my visit may not be appreciated."

"No?"

"That woman is a terror. I'm almost afraid to go over."

"Oh, the hell you are!"

"You know me well. That old skinflint doesn't bother me."

Two more cars, the second one close on the first one's tail, raced down the road, swerving around the moving van. The two women fell silent. A slight breeze touched their hair and carried the sound of voices to them from across the street.

"Mack! Git yer ass out here and help me carry this dresser! Don't be slobberin' before dinner, you lazy slob! I ain't havin' a meal wasted cuz you already gorged!"

A huge, unkempt man emerged from the house, wearing a filthy pair of jeans and a stained white t-shirt. "Keep yer panties on, you ugly old bitch!"

"Aunt Rosie, Brandon took my doll and yanked her head off!"

"Yer doll looks better now! She was damned ugly!"

"You kids are worthless, shut yer stupid yaps and grab yer stuff out of the damned truck before I whip both yer asses!"

Lauren's jaw dropped and she looked at Rita, who nodded affirmation. "Yep. You are hearing what you think you're hearing."

"Where did these people even come from?"

"Beats me. But I can't wait to find out."

"Wow. I wouldn't go over there. I wouldn't want to have to squeal like a pig."

Rita and Lauren looked at one another and, in unison, burst out into hearty laughter. The noise stopped from the brown house across the street as the new family paused and looked over. The hatchet-faced woman searched until she and Lauren made eye contact; then the newcomer's eyes narrowed.

"Oops, we've attracted attention," Lauren said, thinking, *here we go*. She smiled and waggled her fingers. The other woman sniffed and turned away, carrying a box into her house.

"Pay them no mind. I think we're going to have to adopt that attitude, dear. Those poor children, though," Rita said.

"I know." Hearing barking, Lauren checked her own back yard again. Mop had found her. He stood just behind the fence, smiling and panting. "I have to go." She chugged more of her iced tea, then stood and sighed. "You know, I'll have to have a talk with that daughter of mine about spending more time with her dog."

Rita offered a sympathetic smile and grabbed Lauren's hand in her soft plump one and squeezed. "You hang in there, dear. Me, I have to take Bertram over to the sleep clinic in a little while. He's having his testing done tonight."

"Oh? Well, I hope they can find a way to help him."

"Me too, believe me. I'm getting a bit tired of being up all night every night with his restlessness."

"Thanks for the drink, Rita. I'll talk with you later. Let me know what happens when you go over!"

"Oh, you bet I will. Take care!"

Lauren looked over her shoulder and waved.

In her back yard, she spent fifteen or twenty minutes throwing a stick for Mop; then she called him and they went inside. It was time for the evening meal.

Though Mike and Allison had been gone for seven months, Lauren was just now getting the hang of cooking for one. All of her dinner tonight came from the freezer. She tossed one pre-made hamburger patty unceremoniously in the frying pan and an individual vegetable cup in the microwave along with a plate of tater tots, setting the timer but not yet pushing "Start". Junk, Lauren knew, but she had nothing thawed and didn't feel like spending a lot of time on food. And, she thought to herself, *Allie might be gone and I might be getting used to cooking for one, but I'm still eating from my kid's personal menu.*

In the living room Lauren tried to read a few pages of her current romance novel while she waited for her burger to cook. She set the book aside after reading the same paragraphs several times and absorbing nothing of what she had read. She attributed her lack of concentration to the new neighbors' noise, which she could still hear. She knew she wouldn't finish reading the book, anyway. She found it boring and formulaic, just like all of the other romances she had read. It was time to switch to a deeper, more meaningful genre.

She went back to the kitchen, flipped her burger, and hit "Start" on the microwave. A few moments later, she carried her plate and a glass of Pepsi into the living room. There was no point in sitting at the kitchen table to eat. The kitchen was where families gathered.

Lauren no longer had a family.

She sat through *Wheel of Fortune* and *Jeopardy*, then switched over to Netflix and tried to lose herself in a mindless horror flick. She was still unable to focus, however, so she put on reruns from a 90s sitcom.

She left her plate in the kitchen sink and sat on the back steps, watching while Mop did his last run and bathroom break of the evening. The sun had dropped well below the horizon line, and a dewy dusk had fallen. It would be chilly in the wee hours.

"Come on in, Mop!" She closed and locked the back door behind them. She shut the lights off and made her way through the first floor, closing windows and checking locks. She secured the front door last and climbed the stairs to the second floor. She brushed her teeth and changed for bed; then found herself in her daughter Allison's room.

She picked up the framed photograph from Allie's dresser - the same photograph that sat on the shelf in the living room. She lay back against the pillows on Allie's neatly made bed, Mop stretched out beside her.

She examined their faces, Michael's and Allie's, tracing the edges with her finger. They looked so much alike: dark brown eyes with matching hair, fair skin.

"Allie," she said firmly, "You have *got* to spend more time with Mop. And Michael, I fell in the toilet again because you left the toilet seat up. No, I know I left it up when I was cleaning; it wasn't really you." Her voice broke and rose in pitch. "You both need to learn to be more responsible, do you hear?" She held the picture frame against her chest as her body started shaking. "I miss you so much," she sobbed. "I just want you back!"

She cried until she couldn't anymore, and fell asleep on Allie's bed.

* * *

In the dream, she was back at Parkhurst Middle School. She and Michael were late dropping Allie off that morning. Lauren stayed in the car while Mike walked Allie into the school to sign her in. They hadn't yet reached the double doors when the shooting began.

"*POP, POP, POP*!"

"What the?" Lauren looked in her rearview, then the side mirrors. She saw the boy with the gun run past Mike and Allie, who lay on the cement walk. He ran into the school.

"Oh, my God." She gripped the door handle. "*Oh my God!*" she screamed, and pushed the car door open. Leaving it yawning wide, she ran, her heartbeat echoing in her ears.

Michael lay still, his eyes closed. Dark red blood pooled around his head on the sidewalk; there was a bloody hole in his forehead. Allie was moving and groaning. A bright patch of red spread across the material that covered her small chest, staining her pretty white dress with the frilly bib and apron, printed everywhere with the colored outlines of baby giraffes: dark blue, bright red, yellow, green. Lauren dropped to the ground beside Allison, fear pulling her heart from her chest into her throat.

"Allie?"

"Mommy! I feel . . . weird . . ." She coughed a little, and blood overflowed from the corner of her mouth and ran down her cheek, dripping onto the white cement sidewalk.

Lauren grabbed her daughter's hand and moved so that Allie's head lay on her lap. "Mommy's here, Allie, Mommy's here, and you're going to be just fine.

Allison was going to die, though. Hot tears ran in stinging streams from Lauren's eyes and bathed her cheeks.

She offered her little girl a watery smile. "It feels weird right now, but you'll be just fine."

"Mommy?"

"Mommy's here, honey."

"Mommy . . ."

"I'm here, baby, I'm here."

But her baby had drawn her final breath. She closed her eyes for the last time on the first day of spring, beneath the clear blue sunlit sky.

There was no closure. The boy with the gun had shot himself after killing five and wounding thirteen. Two of the dead were Lauren's husband and daughter. The three others included two students and a teacher. Of the wounded, ten were children, two were teachers, and one was a custodian.

The nightmare never ended.

It repeated itself through Lauren's dreams and remained with her throughout each day. It seemed that nothing could erase the images of the blood from her memory, the blood that spread across her daughter's frilly bib and on the white cement beneath her husband's head.

Except for Mop. Her daughter's dog, the English shepherd had been with them since he was a puppy. Lauren began paying extra attention to him. He was the last remaining member of her family, an extension of her baby girl.

* * *

Lauren woke abruptly from her fitful sleep. She moved, and the sensation of the picture frame sliding away from her brought her to a fuller awareness.

She glanced at her digital clock and saw that it was nearly 1:00 a.m.

She recognized the steel guitar of country music, a deep, throbbing bass in the background. The music was accompanied by people shouting and singing drunkenly. She got up from Allie's bed and shuffled down the hall to the window next to the stairs, which looked out onto the street.

"Uggghhhh," she groaned. The newcomers' house blazed with light, while the other surrounding houses had long since gone dark.

"No matter. It's Saturday," she told Mop, who had padded down the hall at her heels. He wagged his tail and gave her hand a brief lick. "White noise, buddy. Let's go."

She turned her box fan up to its highest setting so the calming noise would cancel the racket outside, then pulled back the covers and slipped into her own bed.

The next morning, the young widow woke from a dreamless sleep, sniffling in the stuffy room. The double layers of blackout curtains that covered the windows revealed no hint of daylight, but Lauren assumed that it was past dawn because she was overwarm, which usually foretold of a sunny day. She stretched and yawned, catching Mop's eye. The English shepherd sat on the floor beside the bed, staring at her.

"I see you," Lauren reassured her canine companion. She sat up, threw back the blankets, swung her feet to the side of the bed and planted them on the floor. The glowing blue digits on her clock read 8:17. "After eight o'clock!" She exclaimed. "No wonder you look so sullen! We're late getting up." She used her cell phone to check the weather. "And it's already almost seventy degrees out!"

Mop stood and wagged his tail as his human pulled on a pair of sweats and struggled into a bra, using a complicated method to don it beneath her t-shirt. He followed her to her bedroom window, smiling eagerly with his wide, toothy grin as she pulled the curtains and blinds and opened the window wide to let in the fresh morning air. The dog sniffed as Lauren inhaled deeply.

She followed suit with the front hall window beside the stairs. She stood for a moment, looking at the brown house opposite her own. The moving van was still parked in the street. Why they hadn't parked in their driveway was beyond her. Their yard was littered with toys, belongings, and furniture. *Good thing for them that it didn't rain,* she thought. Just looking over there was enough to bring on a severe headache.

Lauren turned away. "Ready, boy?" Smiling, his big pink tongue hanging out the side of his mouth, Mop extended his front legs, chest to the carpet, rear-end in the air. "Good idea," his human agreed. "A yoga workout is definitely in order."

She padded down the hallway to the bathroom in her slippers; then she and Mop headed downstairs. Lauren exchanged slippers for flip-flops and let Mop out the back door. As was her habit, she checked her backyard gate latch to make sure it was secure, then returned to the kitchen, leaving the screen door propped so that Mop could freely use the doggie door.

In the living room, Lauren slipped her favorite yoga workout video into the DVD player and unrolled her mat. Soon, she was relaxing into beginning *Savasana.*

About half an hour later, she was planted firmly into the *Warrior I* pose when a barrage of barking sounded outside. Lauren cut her focus, but remained in the pose, listening. *Sounds like Mop. But Mop is shut in the back yard.*

More barking.

Come to think of it, she hadn't heard Mop come back in from his morning ablutions to eat his breakfast crunchies. But she might have been too relaxed to notice whether he had come in.

Lauren sighed and slowly reversed out of the pose. *At least I almost finished the workout.*

Brakes squealed in the street.

Now, Lauren ran through the kitchen and down the back steps in her bare feet. Finding the gate standing ajar, she ran through it and up the driveway toward the street. Relief washed through her when she saw Rita Williams, steering Mop by the collar, waddling in her direction.

"What happened?" Lauren kneeled in front of her daughter's dog.

Rita's lips were set in a thin red line. She jerked her head toward the street. "I saw the little girl open your gate and run away with this fool on her heels."

"What was with the car brakes I just heard?"

"Mop was just bounding his merry way across the street and very nearly got hit. But I got him for you, dear!"

"Thank you!" Lauren wrapped her arms around the wayward canine. "You bad boy, you don't just run after any old thing that comes through the gate!" she chided him.

"At least he's okay. Maybe it's time to get a lock for your gate."

Lauren frowned and looked across the street. "Yeah. Maybe it is."

The two women exchanged brief pleasantries and a promise to get together later, and Lauren led Mop into the kitchen, closing the screen door.

"Now you're grounded," she told him. As she ushered him into his kennel, a loud banging sounded from the front door. "What now?"

She opened the door to a scrawny middle-aged woman with dull brown eyes and a hooked nose set in the middle of her bony face. She sported a stiffly unkempt jet-black mullet, a torn, dirty t-shirt, and faded leggings. Upon seeing the lady of the house, the woman launched into a tirade, shaking her fist.

"You better keep that mangy fleabaga yers on yer own sidea the street! Damn near bit my niece! Next time it happens, I'ma shoot it!"

For a moment, all that Lauren could do was stand there, dumb with shock, staring at her mousy neighbor. Then she gathered herself, smiled brightly, and said, "Really? I'm sorry. What was your name again? I didn't catch it when you introduced yourself."

The woman looked confused for a moment. "Uh . . . Rosalie Preacher."

"Rosalie. What a lovely name! First of all, Rosalie," Lauren said in a calm, even voice, "Pounding on your new neighbor's door and threatening to shoot her dog on your first day in the new neighborhood is *not* exactly the best way to make a good first impression." The other woman started to interrupt, but Lauren held up her hand.

"Secondly, I have it on good authority that *your niece* came over here to *my* yard and *unlatched my* gate, letting my daughter's dog out. Thirdly, *my daughter's dog* nearly got hit by a car because of *your* negligence." Lauren stopped to give her neighbor a chance to speak.

"That didn't happen! That's a lie! Who said that?"

"Someone that I trust, who's never threatened to shoot my dog! I strongly suggest that you keep *your family* on *your* side of the street and *out* of my yard. And if I were you I would not touch *one whisker* on that dog, or there is going to be a *big* problem. Now, *Rosie*, I would appreciate it if you would take yourself off of my porch and get back where you belong." She turned and pulled the screen door open.

"Of all the -" Rosalie spluttered. "Listen, *you*-"

"No, *you* listen, because I'm not saying this again. Get off my porch. Leave Allie's dog alone. And if you ever choose to speak to me again, maybe you should think about being a little more civil." Lauren stood and stared at the scrawny, birdlike woman, who stared back, her mouth working noiselessly. Then she simply gave up and walked away, down the steps and back across the street.

In the kitchen, Lauren let Mop out of his kennel. "*That* went well!" She told him. "It's a good thing I did my yoga workout before she came. I really kept my cool, considering she threatened to shoot you. The nerve!"

She suddenly felt drained. It wasn't even ten o'clock yet, and all she wanted to do was go back to bed.

Glancing out the kitchen window, she saw Rita walking across the driveway. She opened the door before the older woman had a chance to knock.

"Hello, dear! I heard the little woman making a big noise over here. Are you all right?"

Lauren sighed and held the door open so that Rita could step into the kitchen. "I'm not my best. I had a rough night. I was just trying to have a nice, relaxing Saturday."

"Is there anything I can do? Have you even eaten yet this morning? Or had coffee? How about I fix you some brunch." She put a hand on Lauren's arm and guided her to the kitchen table. "Sit down."

Mop ran up to Rita eagerly and received a hearty petting and baby talk, then he settled down on his giant pillow in the corner of the kitchen. Rita bustled around, opening and closing the cupboards and fridge, clattering pans and dishware.

Lauren leaned back limply in her chair. "I swear, Rita, I don't know what I would do without you. You're always helping me. Cooking. Cleaning. Watching my back. I give so little in return."

Rita flapped her plump, pale hand. "Honey, *I* don't know what I'd do without *you.* I'm bored as hell over there. Bert's always puttering in the garage or watching sports. Retirement isn't all it's cracked up to be. Actually, it *sucks*. I don't go to bingo or have a book club or any of that kind of stuff. You're like the daughter I never had, and you need me. You've been through hell, and I'm happy to be here for someone. I need to be needed, so it works out perfectly." She poured pancake batter into a hot, greased pan. Then she poured two cups of coffee from the freshly brewed pot and handed one to Lauren, who sipped it gratefully.

"This is so much better than when I make it," she commented. "I don't get it. Same coffee. Same water. Same coffee pot."

"So, like I said, I heard what little Miss New over there had to say. But you were remarkably quiet."

Lauren shrugged. "I was feeling pretty mellow, but I told her off, anyway. She told me her niece didn't come over here, called you a liar, pretty much. Then she threatened to shoot Mop."

Rita turned around, her mouth a big round "O". "You're kidding me," she said in a hushed voice. "What did you say?"

"Told her to go away and leave me alone. Told her to keep her family over there. That's all."

Rita shook her head as she slipped the spatula under a pancake and flipped it. "Well. I don't know what to say. I can't wait to get over there with a pie."

"You still want to go over there with your greeting service?"

"Of course! Especially now. 'Know thy enemy,' dear. If she's going to establish herself as your enemy, then I *really* need to know what she's doing. And to do that, I need to be neighborly. And taking a pie over is a neighborly thing to do."

"Wow. You don't have any underlying motives toward *me*, do you?"

"Goodness, of course not! You're practically family." She set a plate of pancakes and bacon on the table in front of Lauren and took her own place.

"I've been so tired. It would be Allison's birthday next week, and I keep thinking about her."

"Of course you do."

"And when she threatened Allie's dog, I just . . . I'm glad you're here." She took a bite of her meal. "Hey, how did Bert do with the sleep study?"

"They sent him home with an oxygenator when I picked him up this morning. Supposed to help. It's probably just going to be one more thing that will keep *me* from sleeping."

"But maybe it will help him. And if it helps him, it should help you, too," Lauren said positively.

"I can only hope."

* * *

The moving van had disappeared from across the street and the newcomers were quieter than they had been the night before, but the two women decided to take a break from the front porch in favor of the privacy of the Williams' back yard when they reconvened later that evening. As they enjoyed after dinner drinks, Lauren kept an eye on Mop, next door in her own back yard. The breeze had picked up, and the dog frolicked after leaves that blew randomly down from the trees.

She held up the padlock she had bought that afternoon. "Here it is! I had to buy a hasp, too. I'll install it tomorrow."

"I'll send Bert over to put it on for you."

"I can do it myself, Rita."

"Oh, I know you can. You're probably more capable than most men. But it'll give Bert something to do. He likes to feel needed, too, and he can't get enough *real* fix-it jobs. Right, dear?"

"Yes, Rita," the stooped old man said, letting the screen door slam as he stepped out onto the porch. "Wait a minute. What am I agreeing to?" He sat down in one of the porch chairs, set his full beer bottle down, and shook a cigarette out of a half-empty pack.

"Well, for one, that's a beastly, disgusting habit. No wonder you need oxygen."

"No, I need the oxygen because *you* use it all up, gossiping like you do. Scientific research. Peer-reviewed." He gave Lauren a sidelong look and winked one mischievous blue eye.

"Why don't you stop over to Lauren's tomorrow and put up the hasp on her gate."

Bert blew out a plume of smoke and looked at the lock and hasp that lay on the table. "All right. I can do that. Should take all of five minutes." He took a swig from his beer bottle.

"Thank you, Bert!" Lauren grinned at him and gave him an exaggerated wink.

Rita laughed. "Well, the old battleaxe did have an earful to say about you and how rude and mean you are, *young lady*."

"I'll bet."

"She loved the pie."

"Of course, she did! Who doesn't love your pie. Pumpkin?"

"'Tis the season."

"Go on."

"Well, she's thirty-something years old."

"Really? She looks almost fifty."

"Yes, she does look quite worn. The big boy is her brother. They're here from Virginia. They moved to New York because her sister has been hospitalized for some reason, don't ask me why, I don't remember. The kids are her sister's kids."

"Wow. What else?"

"Her house is disgusting. I mean, you always expect mess, clutter, and dust, but hers goes beyond the pale. I *should* cut her some slack, since they just moved in and everything is everywhere, you know? But I don't think that she even cleaned up the house before they moved in. I don't think *anyone* has cleaned that house since old man Lane passed on, bless his soul. I tried to help him out with that, but he was so ornery. Never wanted anyone over there. Kind of miss the old codger."

"Yeah, it was too bad that we lost him. I miss him, too," Lauren agreed.

"So she just got a job a few blocks from here, at GeneSystems. She starts tomorrow night."

"Wow, that's pretty fast."

"Well, that place doesn't care. They always need people, they have a big turnover. So she'll be working eleven at night to seven in the morning. She'll be walking. They don't own a vehicle. She doesn't have a license, and he drove the moving van without one."

"Is that how they got here from Virginia?"

"Apparently."

"But how could they get a moving truck without showing a driver's license?"

"I don't know, dear."

"Huh. What else?"

"That's about it. I cut out all the swearing and et cetera, and that's pretty much what was left."

"You mean you've run out of things to say?" Bert interjected, taking another pull off his cigarette and tapping the ash into a small glass ashtray.

"No, just a temporary lull, Bertram."

"Better enjoy it while I can." He put out the cigarette and sat back. "Nice night."

The three sat in silence for a while, sipping their drinks as the sun went down. Mop presently broke the silence, barking through the fence at Lauren.

"You're being paged," Rita said.

"Yup," Lauren agreed. She had fallen into a reflective state, staring out into the night.

It seemed that her emotions had left her. She felt utterly empty inside, and for that, she was glad. She sometimes felt that it was better not to feel anything than to feel the constant, bruised ache of her emotions.

"Hold on!" She called over to Mop. His ears perked up and he stood watching her, wearing his go-to toothy smile, tongue hanging out of the side of his mouth.

She rinsed her glass in Rita's kitchen sink, then headed home after a brief goodnight to her hosts.

She searched for a new book to read on her tablet, but when she found one, it remained unopened. Instead, she sat numbly in front of the television set, watching some mindless sitcom. After about an hour, she stirred. Mop followed on her heels as she made her evening rounds. Satisfied that the house was locked down, she retreated to her bedroom. With Mop snoozing beside her, Lauren fell into a deep, dreamless sleep.

* * *

In better spirits than she'd experienced in many months, Lauren rounded the bends at Southgate Trail, where she often took Mop to walk. She hadn't been for a good walk in the woods in a while. It felt good to be outside, moving down the cedar-strewn path. She had dressed warmly, as the morning chill had accompanied the advent of deep fall. The air held a new, fresh, clean bite that brought a bright pink flush to Lauren's cheeks and helped to clear her mind.

The English shepherd trotted along beside her. At first, he had bounded around at the numerous chipmunks and squirrels, pausing with his chest to the ground, inviting them to play; but Lauren had quickly gotten him calmed and into the rhythm of the walk, and now he remained at her side as the tiny rodents scattered at their approach.

Human and canine paused at the pond. All seemed quiet, except for life beneath the water's surface. The lily pads shifted as fish, swimming beneath the broad leaves, brushed against them.

At the car, Lauren poured Mop a bowl of water and praised him. "That was a good walk, buddy! We walked . . ." she unhooked her pedometer from her waistband and looked at it closely: "Five-point three-six miles! Over five miles! Good job!" She held out her hand. Mop put his paw on Lauren's palm and she fed him a treat. She knelt and put her arms around the dog's sturdy body. "I'm so glad you're here," she told him, squeezing him until he let out a small grunt. "I really wish Allie and Mike were here to do this with us, though." She let go and looked into his big brown doggy eyes. "You look as sad as I feel, sometimes. I'll bet you miss them just as much as I do." He tipped his head sideways. Lauren ruffled his head with her palm.

Back home, Lauren let him out the back door and checked to make sure the gate was latched. She ran upstairs to the bathroom and started the water running for a bath. Waiting for the tub to fill, she glanced out the window and saw that the sky had grown full of ominous gray clouds. Small drops of rain began to tap against the window. *Better bring Mop in,* she thought.

As she headed down the stairs, a volley of barking and shouting erupted outside. Then Lauren heard the screech of brakes, a loud *thump,* and a high-pitched *"Yipe!"*

"*Lauren! Lauren!*" Rita yelled her name outside.

She took the remaining steps two at a time, beginning to panic, her inner voice repeating, *Oh, my God, oh my God, Mop got hit, Mop got hit!* She burst through the front door and ran outside. The cold, fine rain covered her face in a blanket-like mist.

"*Mop!*" she screamed. She ran to the street, where a mound of black and white fur lay limply on the wet pavement in front of an idling black car. She fell to her knees beside the dog.

"Mop, Mop!" She felt his body, looking for injury. In the glare of the car's headlights, which reflected brightly against the surreal mist, she saw his head, which had taken the greatest impact. The dog's skull looked misshapen. The one eye that she could see was open and lifeless, surrounded by bloody, matted fur and broken fragments of bone. Her voice rose in anguish. "*Noooooo, nooooo*, Mop!"

"Honey, honey!" Rita was beside her. "Don't look, don't look!" The older woman wrapped her arms around Lauren and pulled her to the side so that she blocked the younger woman's view.

"I'm sorry, I'm so sorry, the little boy ran out and the dog was right behind him, I tried to stop, I didn't mean to hurt your dog!" The man's voice cut through Lauren's heartbroken sobbing. She looked up and saw the young man standing just behind his open car door.

"*You!*" she shouted. She stumbled to her feet, shrugging off Rita's embrace, and launched herself at the man. She shoved the car door as hard as she could, slamming him between the door and the car's frame. "*You killed Allie's dog! He was all I had left!*"

"Hey! I'm trying to apologize!" He tried to hold off Lauren's vicious attack as she slammed the door repeatedly against his body.

"You wouldn't have to apologize if you weren't *speeding* down the *road!*"

"Lauren! Lauren, stop! You're going to get yourself in trouble! Bert, help me!"

Bert and Rita dragged Lauren away from the car, and she gave in and turned away. As she did so, she saw Rosalie Preacher standing in her yard across the street. Her sallow face wore a smug, satisfied smile. She patted her nephew's back as she observed the spectacle unfolding in the street.

Rita gave Bert a look, and he responded with a slight nod. He led Lauren back to the Williams' house and into the living room. He gently lowered her on to the sofa.

"You stay right here for a few minutes, okay?"

She simply nodded, unable to speak. She curled up on the sofa, shivering in her wet clothes. Cold water dripped from her hair and ran down the back of her shirt.

Bert went out to his garage and grabbed a tarp. When he returned to the scene of the accident, Rita was talking to the driver of the car that had hit Mop. "The dog belonged to her daughter. Her daughter and her husband were shot in the Parkhurst Middle School shooting this year," she was saying. "You had no business driving so fast through a clearly marked speed zone."

The young man's face tightened with distress. "That's terrible! Now I feel even worse!"

"Do something to help, then," Bert said, beckoning him toward the body of the dog, which lay in the rain on the shiny pavement.

Together, they rolled the body in the tarp. When they were finished, Bert turned around and waved an arm at several of the neighborhood residents that had gathered in the street and on the sidewalk to look on with sympathetic expressions. "You all can go home. Show some respect, already. What, don't you people know enough to get in out of the rain?"

The neighbors disbursed, murmuring quietly to one another. All except for Rosalie Preacher, who continued to smirk as the young man lifted the tarp-wrapped canine from the pavement. Bert stopped and glared at her with laser-blue eyes. Unnerved, she turned away, pulling the boy with her.

"Aunt Rosalie, did the doggie die?" The little girl, Elaine, asked. Her aunt's response was unintelligible as they disappeared into their house.

Bert sighed. He looked at the young man holding the tarp. "What's your name, boy?"

"Jack Phillips, sir."

"This way." Bert led Jack out to his back yard shed, where Jack lay the dog's body down gently on the floor. Bert figured it would do temporarily until Lauren could get herself together.

When the road was empty, the rain washed the blood and bone splinters from the pavement.

* * *

"I brought you some warm, dry clothes from your house," Rita said, sitting beside Lauren on the sofa. "I noticed your bath was running, so I shut the water off. You can take your bath here. I don't want you to be alone right now."

"Thank you," Lauren said in a raspy voice.

"Why don't you go on up? You must be chilled to the bone. You need to get out of those wet clothes and get warmed up."

Only at her friend's mention of it did the feeling of her cold, wet clothes clinging to her skin register to Lauren. She trudged up Rita's thickly carpeted stairs to the bathroom and gratefully sank through the thick layer of bubbles into the hot water. She lay back against the end of the tub, closed her eyes, and tried to process what had just happened.

Gradually Lauren became aware of the murmur of voices. Sitting up slightly, she cocked her head to the side, listening, trying to bring the sound into focus. She looked over the side of the Williams' claw-foot bathtub and noticed the heat vent. Rita and Bertram must be having a conversation in their kitchen, which was located directly below the bathroom. Their voices drifted up through the vent.

"You really think she did it on purpose?" Rita was saying to her husband.

Lauren stilled, straining to hear.

"Rita, I am telling you. I looked out the window because I heard the dog barking, and I saw that woman standing there. She was looking down the street. Then she called to the kid kinda sudden. She was waving, yelling that he had to come home *then,* that he needed to get back across the street right away. As soon as the kid was out of the way, *bam!* That car hit the dog. That's how it looked. Set up at the last minute."

"Well, from what I've seen of her, I wouldn't put it past her. And I saw that smile on her face. That woman was *happy*. *Smug*. What I wouldn't have done to go over there and wipe that smile right off her face! What are we going to do? Should we tell Lauren?"

"You know I don't gossip. I don't make accusations lightly, either. I think she *did* do it on purpose, but I don't think it will help Lauren's situation for her to know that. Who knows how it will affect her? I think we should keep it to ourselves, but behavior like that . . . anyone who would deliberately do something like that – I can't have it. Not so close to where I live. You and I are going to have to figure something out, because who knows what else she is capable of?"

"How am I going to keep it to myself, when Lauren has the right to know? It'll kill me to keep my mouth shut."

"You'll do what you need to do."

But it was too late. Lauren had already heard every word.

Once home, Lauren walked through her empty house to the kitchen. She saw the padlock and hasp lying on the kitchen table. She grabbed the padlock and looked at it for a moment.

"*Fuck!*" she screamed, and threw the lock as hard as she could. Its heavy weight carried it straight through the windowpane, which shattered on impact, falling straight down, the larger shards smashing to smaller pieces when they hit the linoleum.

Only a few seconds passed before Rita was calling her name.

"Lauren? Are you all right?" Rita's red, springy curls appeared on the other side of the broken window. "Oh, shit. Lauren?" She came through the kitchen door, Bert right behind her.

"Oh, honey, oh dear." She held the sobbing Lauren once again. "I can't stand this! I can't stand seeing you this way!"

"You don't have to." Lauren said, the word broken by her sobs, her chest heaving. "You don't need to be here."

"Yes, I do," Rita insisted firmly. "Bert and I are going to fix this for you. Aren't we, Bert?"

"Yep," Bert responded. He was already sweeping up the broken glass with Lauren's kitchen broom.

But neither of them was talking about the broken window.

* * *

Lauren didn't fall into the numb depression she had experienced when she lost Michael and Allison. Her mind worked overtime, thinking about Rosalie Preacher. Cold anger motivated her, propelling her through her subsequent days, during which, when she replayed it over in her head, she kept seeing Rosalie Preacher standing in her front yard with a satisfied smirk on her face, patting her nephew, Brandon, on the back. The more she put that split-second together with the conversation she'd overheard, the more convinced Lauren became that Rosalie Preacher had seen and taken an opportunity to get back at Lauren for dismissing her.

But she couldn't prove it. Her dog had run across the street, excited at chasing a potential new playmate.

Rosalie Preacher had killed her daughter's dog, the last remaining member of Lauren's family. She had no siblings, aunts, uncles, cousins, parents. She had been placed in the foster system at an early age, and had grown up in several different foster homes. One of the only things she had ever wished for in life had been an average, traditional family. With her marriage to Michael and then Allison's birth, Lauren's dream had come true. A real family, with a family dog. Lauren had cherished them all.

Her husband and daughter were taken from her by an angry, confused teenager.

Now, her family pet had been taken by an ignorant, spiteful bitch.

Lauren started making plans.

* * *

Two days after the accident, an unfamiliar number came across Lauren's cell phone display. She normally ignored unfamiliar numbers and sent them to voicemail, but this time, she answered.

"Is this Lauren Lattimer?" A man's voice said.

"Who's asking?"

"I'm sorry, it's Jack Phillips. Um . . . I'm the one who hit your dog."

"What the hell? Why are you calling me? *How did you get my number?*"

"I'm sorry, I'm sorry, your friend Rita told me I should call you and try to help you."

"How do you think you can help me? *You killed my dog.*"

"Like, maybe help with his expenses . . ."

Lauren hadn't even begun to think about arrangements. Jack's phone call was a grim reminder that she had to take care of Mop's body as soon as possible. And then she thought, *he was speeding . . . but he was set up, too . . . it wasn't all him . . .* but it could have been. Even if Rosalie hadn't been there, there was a good chance that Jack would have hurt someone, sometime.

But Rosalie *had* been there, and if it hadn't been for her actions, Mop might still be alive.

But at least *one* of those responsible for his death was coming forward to help. And last rites, even for a pet, were expensive.

She should accept the offer.

"Um . . . okay. I'll send you the bill. You can reimburse me." She took down Jack's address and phone number.

After another two days, Mop's ashes lay in an urn beside the other two on the living room shelf, his framed photograph together with the photographs of Michael and Allison. Lauren had missed the previous four days from work, and decided that it made no sense to return to work on a Friday, so she stayed home one more day.

She didn't tell Rita or Bert that she had heard their conversation. She knew that if anything happened to her and they knew she had overheard them, they would feel guilty and want to take the blame. Lauren didn't want that. What she intended to do was her own decision, and she would accept the consequences of her own actions.

* * *

She wore a black pair of jeans, black sweatshirt, black jacket, and sneakers. The autumn nights had grown colder; a good excuse to tuck her long brown waves into a black winter cap. When she got home from work every day, she ate a small meal and went to bed to try to catch a couple of hours of sleep so that she could be awake and alert at 10:30 p.m. – right when Rosalie Preacher left on her lonely evening walk to work.

Lauren watched out the window from her darkened bedroom. When she saw Rosalie leave her house, she waited five minutes and slipped out her back door, out the gate and up her driveway. Keeping Rosalie just in sight and staying to the shadows, Lauren tailed her every night for the next several weeks.

Lauren found that she could set her clock by the scrawny older woman. She left her house at precisely 10:30 every night. She carried her mid-shift meal in the same light blue lunch bag. She walked at the same speed, took the same route, and reached work at the same time each night.

Lauren also noted another detail that helped her formulate her plan. Rosalie Preacher crossed the Marshall Avenue train tracks just ahead of the 10:53 train.

Without fail.

Lauren decided on the date to fulfill her goal: Halloween. She didn't want to wait too much longer than that. The snow would soon fly, and she didn't need the added complications of footprints leading back to her.

* * *

One dark night, Bert Williams, ever the insomniac, sat in the shadows of his front porch, quietly smoking a cigarette. He wore a knit cap and quilted flannel jacket against the cold.

He had just butted his smoke and was about to open his front door to go back inside when he saw motion from the corner of his eye. He looked on silently as Lauren walked quickly through the shadows, following Rosalie Preacher.

He mentioned his misgivings to his wife over dinner that evening.. "She's up to something. She's going to get herself into trouble."

"Well, what do you want do about it?"

Bert sighed. "I don't know what to do about it if I don't even know what she's doing."

"You know what I think?" Rita tipped the salad bowl and spooned a second helping onto her plate. "If it were *me* in her shoes, I would want revenge." She speared a tomato wedge and popped it into her mouth.

"Yeah?"

"Think about it. Justice was never served with that boy that shot Mike and Allie. Lauren is still dealing with that loss. Then you get that old skinflint over there, scratchy, harsh, ignorant, and mean enough to do what she did, all because Lauren kicked her off of her porch."

Bert sat for a moment, contemplating his plate. He shook his head and looked at his wife. "I don't *want* to think it," he said.

Rita put her plump hand on his thin, bony one. "I don't either."

* * *

When Lauren visited Rita on occasion during those few weeks, secrets hung in the air, invisible, between them. Lauren didn't volunteer any information about her nocturnal activities, and her friend acted as though the only reason for Lauren's preoccupation was the loss of her family pet. Bert said very little about anything, but that wasn't unusual. Lauren didn't notice the glances the couple exchanged.

Rita visited Rosalie Preacher twice more after day of the accident. Because Rita was the neighborhood busybody and none of the neighbors on their block were exempt from her periodic drop-ins, anyone who might have seen her entering or leaving the Preacher house wouldn't think twice about it.

Her last visit was on Halloween afternoon, and Rosalie took a pie with her – an individual pie.

"Now Rosalie, honey, you'll want to eat this pie up all on your own. Don't share it, it's a gift just for you. And make sure you eat it *tonight*, after dinner. This brand of pumpkin spoils quickly, so you can't let it sit long, at all."

Rosalie Preacher obliged and ate the pie while Mack took Elaine and Brandon trick-or treating.

That evening, Lauren went over to help Rita hand out candy. The trick-or-treaters came and went, some in large groups, some in-between stragglers. Most of the parents stayed down by the sidewalk, allowing their children the illusion of independence. Others whose kids were still toddlers accompanied them to the door, coaching them on how to push the doorbell or knock on the door and yell "*Trick or treat!*"

As the hour grew later and the throng slowed to a trickle, Rita looked at Lauren's wan face with concern. "Are you all right, dear?"

Lauren shook her head, her hazel eyes brimming with tears. "I should have been out there with Allison tonight."

Rita put an arm around her. "I can't even begin to imagine how this must feel to you. I wish that I could help."

Lauren was silent.

"Would you like to stay with us tonight? There's no reason for you to be alone. Why sit home by yourself?"

"Oh no, that's okay. I wouldn't want to impose."

"Are you sure, dear? We're right here. We have the room. We would love to have you as an overnight guest. Right, Bert?"

"Yep," Bert said from the armchair where he sat watching *Jeopardy*.

"See? Stay with us, Lauren, please. There's no reason to leave."

"Thank you so much, Rita, I really appreciate your offer. And I know you're trying to help, but tonight I kind of feel like I need to be alone."

"Okay, but we're right here if you need us. For anything at all. Okay?"

"Yes, thank you. You've been a wonderful friend to me, and I am really grateful. I'll probably see you tomorrow."

Rita forced a smile. "Of course, you will, dear. Have a peaceful night."

After the door closed behind her young friend, Rita turned to her husband. "You're tagging along tonight, right?"

"Yep."

"Can you say anything besides 'yep'? I'm afraid for her."

Bert turned and looked around the side of his armchair. "Don't worry. I've got it covered. You did your part, I'll do mine. It'll work out all right."

"Are you sure?"

He grasped her hand as she came to stand beside him. "Positive."

She sat on the arm of his chair and leaned over to hug him. "Aw, Bert, I knew there was a reason I married you."

"Got that right."

Wanting to be alert and refreshed for her evening's activities, Lauren napped for a couple of hours. By the time she woke up, the trick-or-treaters had dispersed and most of the houses on her section of Blackberry Lane were dark.

She dressed carefully, tucking her brown waves up into the wig cap before arranging the short wig upon her head. It was a man's hairstyle. She taped the bulky padding around her midsection and thighs. She pulled on Michael's old nondescript gray-blue sweatshirt over a thermal shirt and long-sleeve t-shirt, and completed the outfit with a pair of his blue jeans. She hadn't yet been able to bear sorting and donating his clothes. His larger clothing accommodated the extra padding.

She donned a pair of old platform boots that added two inches to her height while retaining stability and balance. She had considered wearing a fake moustache and a baseball cap to further disguise herself, but decided against it, thinking that too many props would make her more identifiable. Instead, she went subtle and used brown-tinted contact lenses over her hazel eyes and opted for a little fake stubble. *Less is more.*

Anyone who might have seen Lauren as she walked down Blackberry Lane that Halloween night would have described her as an average white man, twenty pounds heavier and two inches taller than she actually was.

The night was chill and empty as she slipped after her prey. It was easy to keep to the shadows. Clouds had created a canopy that obscured the moon and stars, leaving the street cloaked in darkness, except where big yellow circles pooled beneath the streetlights.

Rosalie Preacher didn't seem to sense the presence behind her. On the evenings that Lauren had previously tailed her, the sharp-faced woman had never so much as looked backward over her shoulder. Tonight was no different, except that Rosalie Preacher walked a little slower than usual . . . and there was a slight weave to her gait that Lauren hadn't noticed before.

She kept an eye on her surroundings as she moved along, making sure that she was unobserved. Except for the occasional passing car, there was no traffic. She could feel the rumble of the approaching 10:53 train vibrate from the ground, up through her feet.

Its horn brayed through the crisp night air.

She stopped at the brick corner of the now-defunct train station. This part of the street was unlit. She looked around, checking that the surrounding environment was empty of witnesses. She took long, slow breaths, trying to remain calm.

Lauren was loud and boisterous sometimes, sure; but she was not normally a violent person. Even though she did harbor negative feelings about some people, she had never truly wanted or planned to bring harm to anyone else – until now.

She gathered her resolve and stepped forward to close the last few feet between herself and Rosalie

Preacher. The train's horn sounded, coming closer every second. She couldn't hesitate. Rosalie needed to be down on the tracks with plenty of time for Lauren to remove herself from the vicinity and from the view of the train.

But Lauren slowed as she saw Rosalie Preacher stagger, weaving to and fro at the side of the road. Then the woman crumpled to the ground. Lauren hesitated, then ran to her on tiptoe. Rosalie had fallen across the closest rail. Lauren looked down the tracks. The train was less than two minutes away.

She squatted and touched the woman's bony wrist. She was warm and had a pulse. As Lauren bent over the unconscious woman, she caught a whiff of alcohol. Rosalie Preacher was going to work drunk! The woman had put herself directly into the position that Lauren had intended to contrive. She could just walk away and leave this unpleasant human being to the end of her own making. There was nothing to indicate Lauren had ever been there.

She knew that her conscience would weigh heavily on her mind if she took that route. Was she a murderer? If she went through with this, she would be just like the boy that had taken Michael and Allison from her. She would be like Rosalie Preacher, whom she believed had set up Mop's death.

Was she like Rosalie Preacher? Did she want to lower herself to that level? Did she really want to perpetuate this cycle?

The train was drawing near. Lauren had to make a decision.

She hooked her hands in the woman's bony armpits. Knees bent, she pulled, taking several steps backward. She dropped Rosalie Preacher a few feet outside the rail, then scanned the sandy dirt for any marks she might have left, but night's darkness cloaked any footprints or drag marks there may have been.

She was out of time, anyway. She left Rosalie Preacher where she had dropped her and disappeared into the shadows at the back of the old railway station seconds before the train's headlight bathed the crossing with yellow light.

That night, Lauren slept like a baby in her otherwise empty bed.

Bert tossed and turned.

But that was nothing unusual.

* * *

"Lauren, you need to come over!"

"Wha? Why?" Lauren asked sleepily, turning over, cell phone to her ear.

"Just come over! Keep your pajamas on, it doesn't matter, just come over, I'm brewing coffee! I have big news!"

"Ughhhh," Lauren said, clicking the "End" button on her cell phone.

Twenty minutes later, Lauren sat in Rita's kitchen, a steaming cup of coffee in front of her. "So what the hell is going on that you had to roust me at—" she looked at her cell phone, "—Seven-sixteen a.m. on a Sunday morning?"

Rita slapped the Sunday paper down on the table. "Front page news!"

Lauren looked at the photo. "That's the very recognizable face of our new neighbor."

Rita nodded excitedly. "Read!"

Lauren read, her lips moving. "Pronounced dead at the scene . . . mangled body was found lying on the train tracks, appeared to have been hit by an oncoming train. Smelled of alcohol . . . police are investigating . . ." She looked up, her heart pounding, hands trembling.

"Why, honey, you're as white as a sheet! Are you okay?"

"She's dead!"

* * *

"Do you think we should tell her that I planted your pills in Rosalie's bathroom and drugged her pie?" Rita asked Bert over dinner that evening.

"Nope," said Bert, shoveling a forkful of Rita's homemade macaroni and cheese into his mouth. "I wouldn't want her thinking badly of us. Plus her knowing would be on her conscience."

Rita looked worried. "But she's probably scared out of her mind that she's going to be charged with murder."

"But she won't be." Bert shrugged. "It isn't Lauren's fault the woman is a drug addict who took too many pills and got drunk at the same time. There was no evidence anyone else was there. I checked after the train ran through."

"*She* doesn't know that."

"Leave it alone. It'll work itself out. "

A couple of Fridays later, Lauren drove down Blackberry Lane, slowing to steer around the police cars that were parked front of the Preacher house. There were three, plus an unmarked van in the driveway. It looked as though they were getting ready to leave. As she drove past, Lauren saw that there was someone in the back of one of the cars. It looked like Mack, Rosalie Preacher's brother.

She kicked the snow off of her boots as she climbed Rita's front steps. Rita opened the door before Lauren even had a chance to knock.

"Come in, come in, have coffee, get warm!"

Lauren gladly let her friend lead her into the warm kitchen, where the smell of freshly brewed coffee permeated the air.

"Cookies, have cookies!"

Lauren sat and sipped the hot coffee, feeling its heat spread from her stomach, warming her, and the sudden surge of caffeine through her system. "So what's going on across the street?"

"I don't exactly know," Rita said, taking a sugar cookie from the plate she'd set in the middle of her kitchen table. "They arrested that Mack. Cuffed and stuffed him. And the woman, I think she's a social worker, took the kids and put them in the van."

"Wow."

"I don't know why. But it will either be on the local news or in the papers tomorrow. We'll find out."

"Yeah."

* * *

Rita knocked on Lauren's door the next morning. "*I found out!*" She squealed, brandishing the Saturday paper.

"Come in, come in," Lauren yawned. It wasn't yet eight o'clock, so the two began where they'd left off the evening before: with a fresh pot of coffee.

Lauren read the article that Rita shoved beneath her nose. "Kidnapping? Those weren't Rosalie's sister's kids?"

"Nope. Rosalie and Mack took them from Virginia. It isn't the first time, either."

"Authorities are unsure at this time whether the couple abused the two children . . . wanted for questioning in another child's disappearance in Virginia. They were a *couple*?" Lauren shuddered. "Martin Bishop was arrested at his home yesterday . . . children were remanded to the care of Children's Protective Services . . . Robin Bishop's body was found on the Marshall Avenue train tracks, pronounced dead at the scene . . . was under the influences of illegally obtained prescription drugs and alcohol . . . her death has been ruled an accident; no foul play is suspected." She stopped and took a deep, quiet breath.

Rita watched her carefully. "Do you feel better now, dear? I think you may have been worrying that your argument with the deceased might get you into trouble."

"Yes, I was anxious about that. I was worried that they would come and ask me questions."

"But you didn't do anything wrong, right?"

Lauren shook her head.

"Then why worry?"

Lauren shook her head again and shrugged.

Rita cleared her throat and changed the subject. "Have you heard from that young man?"

"Who?"

"You know . . ."

"You mean the one who killed Allison's dog?"

"Well, yes."

"He sent me a check to cover Mop's final expenses."

"*And?*"

"And *what?* I hope you're not asking me what I think you're asking me."

Rita looked sideways.

"You *are! Shame* on you, Rita!"

"Hey, it wasn't *all* his fault."

"His carelessness is what made the situation possible." Lauren could feel her face getting hot.

Rita put her hands up, palms out, in a defensive gesture. "Okay, okay. I just thought maybe . . . and he tried to make it right."

"Money can't make it right. Thank you, but I'm fine."

"I understand, dear." She sipped her coffee. "You're invited to Thanksgiving dinner. Don't bother bringing anything, unless you want to bring some nice spirits."

"Why thank you. Of course I'll come."

"It's been a rough year for you. I hope things will change for the better."

"Thank you for the thoughts. Honestly, I don't know how much more death I can handle. I hope Rosalie's will be the last one, for a while."

* * *

Thanksgiving was a low-key affair. Lauren was fully drained, unable to find much to converse about, despite Rita's prompts. She tried to put a brave face on it and smiled. She wanted to be a good guest.

"You don't have to talk if you don't feel like it, my dear." Rita tapped Lauren's arm. "We know you've been through so much this year. I don't blame you one bit. Just be comfortable."

"Thank you." Lauren curled up in the corner of the Williams' sofa with Rita's hand-made afghan, hot cocoa in hand, reading *Real Simple*, while Rita puttered around the kitchen, making the meal. Bert leaned back in his easy chair, smoking cigarettes and sipping beer while he watched football, uttering an occasional exclamation.

She passed the next few weeks cocooned in silence. She went to work, came home, and watched sitcoms. She had lost the desire to *do* anything. She lay awake for hours at night until sleep, at last, came to claim her in the early morning hours.

A week or so before Christmas, Lauren sat on her sofa, a plastic bin of Christmas decorations on the floor at her feet. She felt numb and empty. The Christmas spirit eluded her.

Why bother? She thought. *It's only me. No kids to enjoy the magic of Christmas, or the pretty lights. No family to put gifts under a tree for. Not even a family pet to buy a bone for. What's the point?*

She re-fitted the plastic lid back onto the bin and secured it firmly.

Someone knocked on the front door. When Lauren opened it, she found only footprints in the fresh dusting of snow on her front porch and a large white box with a Christmas card envelope taped to the top. She looked up and down the street and saw the twin rear lights of a vehicle disappear into the distance.

She brought the box inside. She set it on the floor beside the bin of Christmas ornaments and pulled off the attached Christmas card. She opened envelope and pulled out the card. Inside it was a handwritten note:

"Dear Lauren Lattimer,

> I know that the gift in the box can never replace your little girl's dog. I know that it can never be a substitute for the family that you lost, but maybe it can be the start of a second one for you, or at least keep you company. Remember, this is not your daughter's dog. This one is all yours. You shouldn't be by yourself at Christmas.

Merry Christmas,
Jack Phillips"

A faint scratching noise came from the inside of the white box, whose lid had holes punched in it at evenly spaced intervals. She tore away the packing tape that held the edges of the lid down. She gasped when she lifted the lid and looked inside.

Staring back at her were the bright blue eyes of a fluffy white Siberian husky puppy. A pink satin bow adorned its little neck.

"Ohhhh," Lauren said, lifting the ball of fur out of the box and holding it in front of her. The puppy licked her face with her small pink tongue and wagged her little tail.

Then Lauren felt abruptly indignant. "Of all the nerve!" She exclaimed. The puppy tilted her head and looked at her curiously. "How *dare* he! Doesn't he know he should *never* give a gift of a pet to someone? They might not want it. And to *assume* it would make things all better – for *him*! And how did he know I was home? You could have frozen on the porch." Lauren set the puppy on the sofa, where she fell over and wriggled around excitedly on her back. "You *are* awfully cute, though. I can let you stay today, but then I have to call Jack Phillips and have him pick you up and take you back."

Then she began to worry. What if the puppy was a rescue dog? She couldn't live with herself if she returned a dog that needed a loving home. Wait, what was she thinking? Of course this dog needed a loving home. She wouldn't have landed on Lauren's porch, otherwise.

And what would happen after the puppy was gone?

Nothing. Nothing will happen. I'll be alone again in this empty house.

As she watched the puppy trying to attack her own tail, Lauren felt her heart soften and a warm feeling radiate from the center of her chest. She held out her hand. The tiny canine bounded over to her and licked her hand. Lauren picked the puppy up and hugged it to her chest, where it wriggled to free itself. "Oh my *God*! *Fine,* I changed my mind. You can stay. Let's do Christmas!"

She looked inside the box again and exclaimed, "Wow! He really thought about this!" The box contained a food and water dish, a couple of squeaky toys, a small dog bed, a bag of food, and a leash and collar. "You're all set!"

With her new puppy bounding around among the garlands and child-friendly, unbreakable Christmas ornaments, Lauren assembled and decorated her Christmas tree. She turned the tree lights on and shut the living room lights off.

A cup of hot cocoa in hand and her new puppy on her lap, Lauren settled back in the gentle red and green glow of her Christmas tree lights. She turned on "It's a Wonderful Life".

"Joy. That's who you are," she told the puppy. "Aunt Rita's going to love the crap out of you!"

* * *

Rita let the curtain fall. "Lauren has her new puppy, Bertram!"

"It will do her good."

"Should we tell her that the puppy was partly from us, too?"

Bert put down the paper and scowled at his wife. "We tell her nothing. It's best for her to believe it was all Jack. Don't say a word, you meddlesome woman."

"Of course, you're right. That is best, dear." Rita made a zipping motion in front of her closed lips. "I won't say a word."

Bert glared at her for a moment, then resumed his reading.

THE END

ABOUT THE AUTHOR

Shannon Rae Noble was born and raised Upstate New York. She has been writing since she was in the fifth grade. Her published works to date include 160 works of poetry, fiction, and nonfiction in print and online. When not writing, she enjoys reading, listening to music, and exploring new places. She lives with her youngest child, one pug, one cat, one guinea pig, two parakeets, three fish, and one far too overactive imagination.

To learn more, please visit www.shannonraenoble.com.

Made in the USA
Charleston, SC
23 November 2016